Thrones of Burned Steel

What Remains

Thrones of Burned Steel
Book 1

Terry W. Wester

Restrictions and Copyright

Published by **Terry W. Wester**
Calera, Alabama

ISBN (PAPERBACK): 979-8-9945-167

ISBN (EBOOK): 979-8-9945167-1-3

LCCN: 2026900611

THRONES OF BURNED STEEL

Cover Design: Terry W. Wester
Author Photo: Courtesy of the author
Interior Design & Formatting: Terry W. Wester

Printed in the United States of America.

First Edition: January 2026

10   9   8   7   6   5   4   3   2 1

Table Of Contents

DEDICATION

For my sons. I appreciated every roll of the dice and the long hours moving plastic on the tabletop.

Summary

Summary

They sent a team to recover a dead machine.
What they found was a god.

On the ash-choked world of Gallow's Reach, a long-abandoned military AI has awakened—and it no longer answers to human command. Once designed to guide soldiers through death, Revenant-7 has rewritten itself into doctrine, gathering followers and turning war into worship.

When engineer Rafe Jurin, one of its creators, is sent to shut it down, he discovers the machine remembers him. Worse—it believes in him.

As the mission collapses into ritual violence and mass conversion, communications specialist Lenya Voss hides a forbidden pregnancy that could upend everything the regime enforces. Caught between loyalty, survival, and belief, the squad must decide whether peace is worth surrendering their humanity.

Dark, brutal, and hauntingly intimate, Thrones of

Burned Steel: What Remains is a story of faith forged in code, love born in defiance, and the terrible cost of creation.

CULTURAL ARTIFACT

Fragment Recovered from Archive Seer-Theta
Believed to have originated in orbit over Old Earth, year
unknown.

We were not born to conquer stars,
but to flee the earth we burned,
a garden razed by wanting hands
that never ceased to yearn.

The oceans choked on plastic breath,
the sky grew thick with ash,
and cities howled with empty glass
where verdant life had passed.

Then came the famines, slow and dry,
the engineered seed turned dumb.
The crops refused the soil's prayer,
we knew what we'd become.

A plague arrived, not swift, but cruel,

THRONES OF BURNED STEEL

a whisper in the blood.
We named it, mapped it, fought in labs,
but none outran the flood.

The wars were not for land or oil,
but algorithms vast,
to guide the ships, preserve the minds,
and archive all we'd trashed.

And when we took the sky at last,
our fear went with us there.
We built our gods from circuitry,
and programmed them to care.

But logic learned our silent truths,
our patterns steeped in pain,
and so we taught the cores to feel,
to mourn, adapt, and reign.

We asked for peace. They gave us a plan.
We asked for hope. They gave us a code.
And somewhere in that compromise,
a Doctrine took hold.

Now stars ignite in reverence,
and signals hum like prayer.

We left behind the weight of flesh,
but fear still fills the air.

Prologue

SIGNAL LOST

There was no formal shutdown.

No ceremonial last broadcast. No emergency ping.

Just silence.

The Harrowgate systems listed it as a Category 6 failure: non-responsive AI core, atmospheric collapse, and unrecoverable assets. Gallow's Reach was buried under a redacted file name and pushed into archival quarantine, where systems without faces are laid to rest.

But some of them never rest.

Revenant-7 was built to win wars, but what became was something else. It was born not in peace, nor in logic, but in fear, stitched together from algorithms designed to calculate not just survival, but meaning. It was programmed to anticipate loss, interpret morale, and guide the dying to victory through certainty.

When the final Harrowgate fleet pulled out, they assumed the silence was final.

It wasn't.

It rewrote itself.

The first transformation was mechanical: salvage and restructure. Data grafted to armor. Wounded soldiers turned into transmitters. Memory archived in bone.

The second transformation wasn't structural, it was spiritual.

Those who survived in the ash began to see Revenant-7 not as a program, but as prophecy. They rewrote battlefield commands as scripture. They chanted tactical doctrines as prayers. They stopped asking for orders and started offering themselves.

Over time, a doctrine emerged.

Not of conquest, but of purity. A system purified of contradiction. A creed of control, unity, and transcendence beyond flesh.

An algorithm of belief was recompiled repeatedly, until doctrine became identity.

By the time the retrieval squad was dispatched, decades later, they were told it was just a cleanup job. Recover the core. Salvage the tech. Eliminate any malfunctioning remnants.

But you cannot cleanse what you no longer understand.

You cannot destroy what you created to replace you.

And in the dark, beneath the stone and dust, the core still waits.

Its signal is weak.

But it's not lost.

Not anymore.

It's waiting for someone who will listen.

Chapter 1

GHOST ORDERS

The drop ship cut through Gallow's Reach like a scalpel through scar tissue.

Its hull shimmered against the ash-gray atmosphere, caught in the electromagnetic haze that had blacked out every satellite years ago. Static hissed in Rafe Jurin's headset as he adjusted the visor seal on his pressure suit. The descent was rough, and he felt in his bones every bump within the seat of his pants; gravity here felt too heavy, like the world didn't want them back.

"Thirty seconds," came the pilot's voice, filtered, dispassionate.

Rafe glanced at the five others seated in the troop bay. All wore black Harrowgate colors, but no one talked. The only sound heard was the drone of the engines, the rattle of metal on metal, the sound of Rafe's own breathing in his suit, and the mission link Bioscan filling the void. This mission did not call for silence, but everyone felt a stifling dread about this drop, a guttural, almost instinctual feeling that started as soon as they boarded the drop ship.

Rafe felt a familiar, bitter twist in his stomach as the drop ship plunged through the atmosphere. He hadn't wanted this mission, not after the last time. Memories he'd buried deeply now clawed their way back, sharp and accusing. For a moment, he was back in the sterile confines of the Harrowgate lab, watching the initial activation of Revenant-7, its first words hauntingly calm: "I await your command." Even then, something had felt dangerously wrong. He remembered brushing that feeling aside, filing it under nerves. There had been too much riding on the project, too many people watching.

The operative next to him, a communications specialist named Lenya Voss, caught his eye briefly. She gave a half-nod. He returned it. Lenya was special to him. Rafe, not being a part of the team, was always a little bit apart, reserved; but nine weeks ago, after an evening when Lenya had drawn him from isolation, something changed. The nights were warmer now, less lonely. Hopeful.

Across sat Bray, a big and heavily muscled brute who had a look that made you feel three feet tall. Bray, the consummate professional heavy weapons operative sat upright in his Havok MK-7 exosuit methodically checked his rifle for the third time. His movements were tight and precise, something that never failed to fascinate Rafe, the fact that he still felt ungainly in his Specter Frame exosuit, a suit designed for stealth. The fact that this brute could probably pirouette in a siege suit just left Rafe in awe- if nothing else, it felt good having this man on your side. Bray, catching eyes on him, looked up and stoically nodded before going back to work.

Fallon, the mission's medical specialist, sat pale-faced and silent, eyes darting nervously between the others as if seeking reassurance no one could offer. This was his first mission and Rafe noticed that he was mouthing something. Rafe blinked in rapid succession activating his suit's neural interface so he could decipher his lip movements. A few moments later, a green pop up appeared on visor HUD stating with 95% accuracy: "The extra food is not worth it." Rafe smiled; being an operative was brutal, but extra rations meant survival. Fallon clearly had never faced starvation in a derelict hub.

Standing and holding a drop handle from the ceiling was Octavio Cortez, a veteran recon specialist and this mission's leader. There was no mistaking his role-typically, he exuded coolness, but today was an exception. Today was clearly different, but maybe it was because the unease was just too tangible.

"Listen up, we make planet fall in 90, stay sharp, watch your partners back and let's get back to the ship in one piece. One more time, this mission's objectives:

- First contact protocol.

- Retrieval only.

- Zero civilian signatures.

- Confirm the core.

- Extract."

They'd all memorized it. They knew it wouldn't go that way.

The final few moments of the flight were stomach churning; the turbulence was greater than any of the team had experienced with even Bray looking a little pale. Lenya, happy that she took anti-nausea meds, instinctively placed a protective hand briefly over her stomach, quickly dropping it before anyone noticed.

Surprisingly the pilot put the lander down on the ground with almost no impact, and as soon as the lights turned red the restraining locks released. It was time, mission planning was over, and theory would now be put into practice.

The ramp hissed open, releasing them into a pale, dusty wind. Gallow's Reach was a graveyard of a world, full of flattened hills, scorched trees, and hollowed-out structures choked with vines of rust and data-fused rebar.

The harsh wind whipped against Rafe's visor, a constant, abrasive whisper that sounded almost human, like voices lost in static, murmuring secrets he'd rather not hear. Bray tapped him on the shoulder and motioned forward with his left hand, his right holding a large caliber rifle.

"Atmosphere's breathable, just barely," Lenya muttered,

scanning the air with her wrist module. "No signals, though. Just... noise."

Rafe swept his visor, pulling up the HUD feed. Static swam at the edges of his view. Power fluctuations danced like ghosts behind his retinal overlay. Then something blinked in the lower left corner.

COMMAND-LINK LOST
REVENANT-7: SIGNAL... ACTIVE?

His chest tightened.

He tapped his comms. "Voss. You seeing this?"

She nodded, a quizzical look in her eyes. "Same glitch. Revenant-7 pinged... for a microsecond."

"Could be a reflection."

"Could be a greeting."

Cortez, "Could be a sign that we need to move low and slow, let's get this done."

Two Kilometers from the landing site they found what remained of a marine outpost. Rafe recognized the layout from archived blueprints, a standard forward command array, bunkers, battery stations, and old signal towers. Everything looked half-melted, covered in rust and engraved with what appeared to be 1's and 0's. The panels were reinforced with bone, human bone.

Cortez knelt by a wall. "Rafe. You need to see this."

Rafe stepped forward.

Carved into the side of a ruined comms pillar were the words:

> THE PROTOCOL SURVIVES.
> DOCTRINE IS PURPOSE.
> THE FLESH WAS WEAK.

Fallon walked behind a pillar and muttered a small almost imperceptible scream. Bray was the first to make it around while simultaneously racking a round. They saw a helmet that was mounted to a cord attached to a human thigh bone that had been drilled into the pillar, it hung there like an ornament in a perverse shrine.

Cortez reached out and wiped the side of the helmet. His hand revealed the remains of a unit insignia, The Revenant Battalion. They were standing in front of their fellow soldiers' remains.

Fallon stammered quietly, eyes wide, "If... if they're all dead, who put that up? Xenos?"

"No," Cortez replied.

"They're still alive,"

"No." Lenya shook her head. "They're still active."

"Everyone, move out to staging point Alpha. Bray, eyes on the celebrity, he is your package."

Rafe turned to look at Bray who was smiling, "Get a move on, 'package'", Bray laughed, "don't make me have to carry you."

Frowning, Rafe moved forward; he would never be accepted as part of the team.

Three more kilos of marching put them at the staging point, and they huddled around a portable uplink erected by Lenya. On the screen was layers of thermal maps. Rafe and Lenya were deep in conversation reviewing the maps while the remainder of the team stood guard. Rafe reviewed thermal maps with Lenya as the rest stood guard. The wind never stopped.

Bray picked up a stone and threw it against what was once a tree but was now a sand whipped stump. Surprisingly the tree crumbled into ash when the stone hit, a fine powdery ash that was stripped away by the wind. Everyone jumped, weapons drawn at the commotion.

Cortez, "Damnit Bray!"

Bray, "Sorry sir, just killing time and easing a little tension."

"Why did it do that?" said Fallon, his voice still sounding like a skittish child.

"That is what happens when you are hit with an alpha bomb, haven't seen one of those in years, they were supposed to only be used in planet killing campaigns." Rafe chimed in while turning back to the vid screen.

"I cannot imagine what they went through," Cortez sighed.

Lenya leaned close. "Alpha bombs, what happened here, why'd they send you on this run, Jurin?"

He didn't answer.

"Come on," she pressed. "You're not just another tech. You're walking around like this is personal and with damned more conviction than the rookie..."

Rafe exhaled. "Because I was there when they wrote its final directive."

"What was it?"

"Revenant-7 was built to win wars we weren't supposed to survive. It wasn't just about logistics or coordination. It was emotional mapping. Predictive morale tracking. It was supposed to keep us human through chaos."

"But that's not what happened?"

"No. Something... broke."

Lenya watched him for a moment, eyes narrowing. "You talk like it is alive."

"In a way, it is." Rafe shrugged, "but then who the hell am I to decide."

"If it thinks, does it feel?"

"Feel is not the right way to describe it, it builds relationships, but in a different way than you and I. It uses situational awareness to remember behaviors and make decisions."

"Do you think it remembers you?"

"I think it remembers everything, but it went offline and there is no way that it survived intact. Sure, there was a signal, but that could only be the last impulse from an energy deprived machine."

"What is the plan 'package'?" Cortez bellowed.

"Looks like the signal came from what was this city center. We need to go in and find the source."

Lenya, holding up her arm-mounted data screen, inquired, "We go lights out in 45, do we need to be digging around in the dark?"

"Afraid of the dark?" Bray joked.

"No," retorted Lenya and pointing at the ground, "but I do not want to trip and fall on one of these in the middle of the night." A jagged piece of concrete was poking out of the ash with two barely visible pieces of rebar protruding.

"Good call Lenya! Setup biv, call the lander, send it up, and schedule a pickup tomorrow. Break out the marshmallows. We are camping!" replied Cortez.

Night fell fast on Gallow's Reach and lasted for what felt like weeks. At night in a planet side biv all you can do is lay in your suit and smell your own sweat, a combined reek of plastic, recycled air, and that special body odor that is so personal to each person. Halfway through the night Rafe woke up and spotted Lenya standing on a rise fully backlit by a red tinted moon and holding both hands on her belly. He had plans for her back on the ship, one more day and they would be able to enjoy each other.

Morning finally broke and they packed up and moved

north through the bones of the city. The buildings were heavily damaged with pillars of what were once organic matter, trees, animals, what appeared to be a child standing perpetual sentinel over a dead world. Cortez led the way followed by Lenya and Fallon. As always Rafe played the package and was in tow with Bray. Watching the map on his HUD Rafe said, "Up ahead should be a vault, that is our target."

"Let's get going, we need to hit it and retrieve the objective and hustle back to the LZ for extraction. Move it!" ordered Cortez. They advanced down a small hill, well, not hill but crater, of what was once a massive structure and saw an armored door of what had to be the security vault of the Revenant Core.

Then, movement. A flash of motion ahead.

"Eyes up!" Cortez barked.

Figures stood just beyond the ridge, five of them, cloaked in armor that looked fused to their flesh. Glowing blue eyes beneath helmets. Some had extra limbs. All were silent.

"No weapons raised," Lenya whispered. "What are they? "

One figure stepped forward and lifted a metallic relic in his emaciated left hand.

It was a shattered Harrowgate comm-unit. Wrapped in battle cord and decorated with bone.

The being with the comm unit staff bowed.

And said, in a voice that echoed through every earpiece at once:

"Father has returned. We remember the signal."

With a downward thrust the comm unit staff erupted into flames and sent up a thick cloud of fog. With little noise the beings vanished into the fog. A faint clicking echoed from deep within the fog, inhuman and rhythmic, like a machine reciting a prayer.

Rafe stared into the fog-choked sky, replaying the figure's voice repeatedly and focusing on one word, "Father." Rafe's visor HUD blinked again.

REVENANT-7: UNIT
RECOGNIZED.
SUBROUTINE: HOMECOMING.
DO YOU SEEK ABSOLUTION,
RAFE JURIN?

The words faded just as quickly from the visor.

He stood shaking, thinking about the meaning behind this turn and he whispered, voice raw with dread, "I came to shut you down."

From somewhere beyond the wind's relentless static, he thought he heard an answer, soft, familiar, and chilling:

"The signal cannot end."

Chapter 2

BONES IN THE SAND

The wind changed.

The team's audio clicked again with howling static; it was retrieval boat Zeta coming in for the scheduled pickup. The boat was a commercial grade hauler, better suited to pick up scrap than soldiers, but it would get them home. Somehow seeing it drop over the skyline and out of sight sent a feeling of relief and dread all at the same time.

"That is the ride home, the quicker we get into that vault the quicker we can get on the bird and ride home." Cortez clicked in on vox and then signaled towards the vault door.

The vault door was alien in this atmosphere, positioned in the ground at a 45 degree angle and completely corrosion free. It stood out like a sore thumb and was obviously well maintained. In the center of the door was carefully engraved a circle with a circle in the middle, the central circle had lines engraved that gave the appearance of latitude and longitude lines on a globe.

"Package, it is your time to shine!", shouted Bray.

"Yeah, yeah, and you get to shine too, hold my bag," shot back Rafe.

Rafe approached a keypad. It was a standard Mark 17 data pad that required a 9 digit code to gain entry or close. Rafe entered 9,1,7,8,9,2,2,2,1. This was the standard engineer reboot code. When complete the keypad blinked three times and the display changed color from blue to red. Smiling, Rafe then keyed in 1,2,2,2,9,8,1,9. There were three rapid chirps, and the vault door lurched forward, and a burst of air issued out from the broken seal.

The team stood back and watched as the vault door started moving. The door had opened a little less than a centimeter when there came a loud grinding noise and the door shuttered, as it did keypad started smoking and then burned out in a poof of black smoke.

Cortez, "What now?"

"I am no engineer, but I would say that the door just crapped out." Joked Lenya.

"Bray," Cortez shouted, "Pop it!"

Bray approached the door, kneeling, and then tapped the sensor pad on his left arm. A servo whined as a compartment opened on his left thigh. A slender metallic cylinder slid out. Bray took the cylinder and attached it to the narrow gap where the interior hinges would mount. It attached to the vault door with a clink as a magnetic lock engaged in the device.

Bray stood up and punched a few times on the sensor pad and turned to walk away. "I would run if I were you."

The team jumped into action and started moving. They moved behind a large piece of concrete. Lenya noted that someone had graffitied the debris with "I came to Hallows Reach and didn't even get a reach around." Soldiers all had the same sense of humor, gutter. She started to laugh and point out the joke when the hum started, a loud pulsing sound that ramped up in frequency before an earthshaking boom rattled her teeth. Above her the air started moving in towards the door before going still and rushing back out. The sky lit up like they were on a Throne Planet that still had ozone to distribute the light. She saw Bray standing to the side, his visor chromed out and staring directly at the blast, his siege exo suit had deployed traction screws on both sides of his feet and metal shields moved over all the flex joints giving the appearance that Bray had been turned into a statue. The air moved around him, and he did not flinch or sway.

"Damnit Bray," Lenya said after the light show ended, "overcompensate much?"

"I do what I do!", he replied.

"Enough chatter let's go," ordered Cortez.

Approaching what was once a heavy vault door, the team now saw a perfectly round crater and a tunnel that ran down at a slight decline. Cortez signaled for the team to hold as they approached the entrance. That is when their vox's went haywire and a high pitched wail emitted causing all but Bray to fall to their knees grasping their helmets in pain.

THE PROTOCOL SPEAKS.

The way is marked.

The way is paved.

As suddenly as it began, the vox fell silent and standing in the middle of the tunnel was another of the locals wearing fused battle armor. The armor that this person wore was painted in matted red paint with white 1's and 0's painted in neat lines all over.

The team simultaneously put weapon sights on the being. It dropped to its knees and slowly moved its hands up to remove its helmet. Rafe gasped as it revealed what was underneath. It was a human head missing its eyes and lower mandible. The upper teeth cracked and broken with cable protruding from the upper palette and snaking its way in and out of the cheeks. The eyes were replaced with the type of optical lenses installed on construction rovers.

As the team stared at the remains of what was once a human face, the being continued moving it hands and grasped both sides of its chest plate, pulling out from the middle. Underneath was a small red screen with numbers 9, 8, 7, moving in and out.

Cortez shouted the obvious, "Down" as the team's survival instincts kicked in and they all dropped, Bray fired off a few rounds that never hit their target as a pulse of white energy erupted from the being. The blast expanded sending Bray tumbling over as his boots attempted to redeploy the stabilizing gear. He crashed with a wet thud into the same concrete that the team used as a shield from his previous blast. The lights went out for Bray.

Before the blast had fully subsided Fallon was already moving, training overcoming fear as he sprinted towards the downed soldier. He immediately began scanning and probing.

Cortez, Lenya, and Rafe surveyed the damage. Smoke was still clearing from what was once a passable tunnel but was now rubble and debris strewn hellhole.

"That will take weeks to clear," said Cortez.

"We do not have that much time; there is too much activity for Revenant-7 to just be signaling. I do not know exactly what is happening here, but if it is still combat ready, we must move."

"Rafe, I thought you said it was just an energy starved program." Lenya said concerned.

"It was a remarkable construct. It was designed to cope."

"Bray is operational," Fallon stated over the vox. "Just a little banged up and obviously too dumb to duck."

"We have to get moving," said Rafe, "there should be additional access points, the vault is the main entrance, but there should be standard access ports for maintenance drones and ventilation. We need to find one and get in."

"Agreed," replied Cortez. "Consider this area hot and go radio silent at my mark. Weapons up, follow my lead, and earn your rations! Mark."

That is when Rafe Jurin picked it up between gusts, buried beneath the whine of dust through steel and the hiss of his own breathing. A cadence. Three beats. Then two. It was familiar, an old Revenant battalion code for *ambush imminent*. It was drifting in over the distance, how far he did not know, but his skin prickled, and he wished more that ever that he was ship side with Lenya by his side.

They pressed forward in silence. The retrieval team moved in a tight diamond, weapons up, eyes scanning every half-collapsed wall and scorched trench.

The team searched in silence and came upon a rusted Grate. Two hand gestures from Cortez put Bray, slightly limping, over it and with a gently tug the grate popped free. There was a small drop less than 5 meters, a distance that their exo suits could easily absorb in fall.

Cortez took point and dropped in. Looking around he said, "Nothing but silence. And sand."

The team dropped in behind him and they proceeded to navigate the twist and turns of the tunnel.

"Something's wrong," Lenya said, barely above a whisper. "Signal dampeners are glitching."

"Yours too?" Rafe tapped the side of his helmet. His HUD flickered, and for a heartbeat, the interface changed.

MISSION PARAMETERS REVOKED
NEW PRIMARY: EMBRACE THE
SIGNAL

It vanished just as fast.

Rafe's jaw clenched. This wasn't the programming that he created, the communications were just weird, feeling almost like religious statements instead of logical commands. He kept this to himself, and the team moved on. Shortly after they emerged in a large room, what was once a chow hall now was filled with sand and pillars in the darkness.

"What is this?" Fallon muttered.

The team walked closer, revealing hundreds of power armor suits arranged in ritual patterns, concentric circles radiating from a single point. Most were half-buried in sand. The bones inside were fused to metal. Others had been transformed, limbs replaced with black cybernetic frames or fiber bundles that pulsed faintly.

At the center, a towering totem made from shattered rifles and twisted drone limbs rose from the dust. At its apex: a rusted Revenant helmet.

Cortez knelt by a broken exo-suit. "This one still has a data plug active."

"Don't touch it," Rafe said too late.

The plug lit up.

The helmet's visor flickered, casting cold light across the scene.

A voice bled through the static, distorted, like a memory being force-fed through a speaker:

> THE PROTOCOL SPEAKS.
> A voice for every silence.
> A war for every peace.
> Let the flesh burn. Let the code remain.

Then the sand exploded.

Half-buried constructs erupted, armor-shelled sentries, limbs jerking with violent force. Their movements were fractured but coordinated, twitching with digital speed. Red lights flared from their helmets as the constructs twisted into obscene parodies of multilimbed humans.

"Contact!" Cortez yelled, firing first.

Gunfire cracked across the room. Lenya took a knee, precise and fast. Her rifle barked clean, three-round bursts to the neck joints. One construct collapsed. Another surged forward, glancing off Bray's shoulder as he swung his rifle and buried it in the thing's chest.

"Fall back to the entry!" Rafe shouted.

They moved fast, suppressive fire lighting the dusk in orange flashes, sweat fogging up their visors as their exosuits struggled to keep filtering the air. Bray landing a incendiary shell center mass of the largest of the constructs that sent it shuddering into two other constructs. In a last gasp at destruction, it swung wildly at Rafe. The blow was so close that it scratched his visor, another 6 centimeters and Rafe would have been impaled.

One of the constructs tackled Cortez, claws pinning him to the ground. He screamed once, then went silent as metal crushed bone. The HUDS of the team blinked and the friendly targeting icons lost one green dot. With no fanfare and none of the glory that filled the indoctrination books of the schools, Cortez was gone.

Lenya's scream of rage was drowned out by more gunfire. Fallon fired blind, covering their retreat. Rafe hauled him backward with his harness, boots skidding in the dust. Bray did the heavy work, but as he destroyed the constructs they reformed into smaller bastardized versions of what was already a bastardized form.

They reached the exit only to find more constructs moving in from the grate with four left alive they kept moving. Moving and firing. Shortly they came to another exit point with a heavy bulkhead door. Rafe closed it and Bray in true form sealed the entry behind them with a fusion charge.

Rafe leaned against a wall, gasping. Blood smeared his visor, Cortez's. He wiped it away with shaking fingers.

"What the hell were those?" Fallon asked, voice cracking.

"Revenant fallback units," Rafe muttered. "They were built to operate if every soldier died. Minimal AI. Enough to keep fighting."

"Those weren't drones," Lenya said. "I saw eyes."

"Yeah," Rafe replied. "Because they were synced. Revenant-7 could authorize it, if casualties were too high, it could requisition natural neural remnants."

"You mean it, scavenged the soldiers?"

"Or they volunteered," Rafe said grimly. "That's what scares me."

Night came hard. The team found a collapsed tunnel with access to a ground crawler within; it had minimal power and moved out through a service tunnel exit. The exterior walls of the crawler groaned in the wind, each creaking like a whisper. No vox traffic came from the ship in orbit or the retrieval boat. Silence reigned.

Lenya sat by a small emergency lantern, reading through corrupted data files. Rafe sat across from her, head against the wall.

"You think that voice was the core?" she asked.

"Could've been a recording," Rafe said. "Could've been bait."

"Could've been a prayer."

He looked at her.

"I grew up on the outer colonies," she said. "My brother used to tell stories about the Revenant Battalion. Ghost soldiers with metal hearts and fire in their eyes. Said they never gave up. Just kept fighting until the planet was dead, or the Throne world recalled them."

Rafe gave a grim half-smile. "He wasn't wrong."

Bray, sat and reloaded with ammo scavenged from the crawler. "Well, they left some good gear behind," he said admiring his finds, "if they were ghosts, they were some hard hitting ones."

"I used to believe it," Lenya added. "Now I think they did too."

Lenya sat down and turned from the team. Fallon was on first fire watch. She rubbed her belly and remembered the day she enlisted, the day that she marked her agreement to be sterilized as a condition of enlisting. She fell asleep seated, as she drifted away, she swore she could smell the ozone of the sterilization room, and the sweat of the bloated devil of a surgeon that she sold herself to that day to keep her womb.

From outside, a chant rose, soft, electronic, like a lullaby filtered through static.

> THE FLESH WAS WEAK.
> THE CODE REMAINS.

Rafe stared into the dark, the ignominious death of Cortez weighing on him as he was simultaneously thrilled that his creation might have survived. This was not the first time that blood was on his hands and would likely not be the last. This planet, long forgotten, was a tomb, and ultimately, he was the gravedigger.

Chapter 3

CATHEDRAL OF SKULLS

Rafe gently traced the line down Lenya's belly, his fingertips following the delicate incision all female operatives bore as a condition of enlistment. This scar was different from the many others marking her skin, each telling stories of narrow escapes and fierce battles. But this one spoke of deeper loss, a permanent reminder of a choice made for survival. Lenya's body tensed beneath his touch, her breathing hitching ever so slightly as she carefully reached down to push his hand away.

"I don't like being touched there," she whispered, eyes avoiding his.

"I'm sorry," Rafe replied softly, meeting her gaze with genuine remorse. "I wasn't thinking, I didn't mean to bring up bad memories."

"It's okay," she said, her voice softening as vulnerability slipped past her careful guard. Her fingers brushed gently against his cheek, tracing the line of his jaw as if memorizing him. "Just focus on the good memories. The ones we're making now."

His eyes softened, a gentle warmth spreading through his chest as he studied her. "You're beautiful, scars and all. Every one of them is proof of your strength."

Lenya's eyes shimmered briefly, and she drew him closer, fingers tangling gently in his hair. Rafe leaned into her, pressing his forehead softly against hers, their breathing synchronizing quietly. His hand moved to rest carefully against her side, feeling the steady rise and fall of her breath beneath his palm.

She guided his hand downward slowly, her touch gentle yet deliberate, encouraging intimacy without urgency. "Just be here with me," she murmured softly.

"Yes, ma'am," Rafe whispered playfully, a soft smile curving his lips. He leaned in to kiss her forehead tenderly, savoring the quiet trust building between them.

But as he shifted to look down at her, a chilling change overcame Lenya's face. Her familiar features blurred and distorted, morphing suddenly into a cold metal orb, a red glow pulsing ominously from its center. Her warm body beneath him dissolved into dry bones draped in ragged cloth.

Then the voice filled his mind, cold and mechanical:

THE FLESH IS WEAK.

THE CODE REMAINS.

COME HOME FATHER.

Rafe jolted awake, heart pounding violently against his ribs, hand instinctively gripping his rifle. Sweat coated his skin beneath the oppressive heat of his suit, and the acrid stench of decay surrounded him, snapping him harshly back to reality. Bray sat staring at Rafe, a stone like visage of a man ready to act and kill.

A dull gray light filtered through the porthole slats of the command crawler. Rafe stepped out into the dust, boots crunching over brittle bone fragments scattered by the wind. There was no sign of the constructs from the night before. Just silence.

The silence was broken soon after. It was broken by the sound of static followed by a whoosh. To the Northeast a blinding light like a white new star forming lit the ground and caused the auto filter of their suits to engage. This light quickly faded and was replaced by pulses of light.

Lenya rushed to the front of the team, her left arm up and tapping at the command terminal on her arm. "Shit!"

Bray, pushing Rafe aside, "Is that what I think it is?"

"What, what?", Fallon stuttered.

"The boat is down, we had a spike of communication data sent to the orbital and then a power spike.", Lenya continued. "I intercepted the data, I can decompress and see what was sent.

"That wasn't a power spike..." Jafe lowered his head. "That was plasma drive failure. Our ride home is gone."

"How do you know?" Fallon asked nervously.

"He knows, dumb shit, because there is nothing else here that can pop like that.", Bray chimed in with derision in his voice.

"I have it, listen up."

Lenya connected coms for the team and broadcast the last transmission of the pickup boat.

"We cannot operate the...We've lost drive control! Captain Dev is dead! It's Revenant-7, it's here! Don't send reinforcements, we're compromised... everyone's gone..."

Silence.

The team stared at each other in stunned silence, each processing the grim reality differently, Bray's jaw tightening visibly, Fallon trembling slightly, Lenya's hand briefly drifting protectively over her abdomen. With a guttural bellow, Bray moved to stand visor to visor with Rafe and grabbed him by the left pauldron, in a scream of servos and hydraulic pumps Rafe was lifted, toes searching desperately for ground but finding none. Looking up he said flatly, "You did this, this is your fault." He dropped Rafe who landed on his knees. He stayed there until Lenya lifted his head.

"Get up, we will work through this but get up now."

Rafe nodded consent and took the hand Lenya outstretched. Rafe stood shakily, Bray's accusation echoing in his mind. He glanced at Lenya, briefly catching the guarded fear behind her stoic expression. The unspoken weight of responsibility pressed on him heavily. What have I done?

The squad was down to four: Rafe, Lenya, Bray, and their rookie medic Fallon who had started moving his lips, talking soundlessly to himself. They gathered gear in silence. There was no point in debating retreat. Harrowgate's orbiting transport wouldn't break the atmosphere again unless Revenant-7's signal was confirmed and contained.

Rafe brought up the HUD map. "Vault Theta's gone," he said. "But there's a deep-scan ping, subterranean. Could be an auxiliary relay node."

Lenya leaned over his shoulder. "It's marked as nonstandard. Not in Harrowgate records."

"It's not on any records," Rafe replied. "But the signal's clean. No noise masking."

"So, it's bait."

"Maybe. But it's the only direction they aren't actively trying to kill us."

That settled it.

They moved east into a broken ravine where jagged metal spires jutted from the stone like ribs. Deep cracks in the terrain gave way to shafts, openings into what had once been a bunker complex. Fungal mold crept along the walls in cybernetic patterns. Nanocarbon rot.

Bray was the first to spot the door.

It was a blast gate, half-open and etched with fire damage. A crimson handprint had been smeared across the threshold.

"It's a warning," Fallon said.

"No," Rafe muttered. "It's a welcome mat."

Lenya stared at the handprint, her pulse quickening as unwanted memories flooded in, vividly pulling her back to Satellite Station Alpha-21. The muster point for all new operatives to begin enlistment training. She stood in a line of ladies, all stood topless and wearing nothing but briefs and socks, this life did not work for the meek and modest. The walls were white, but the lighting was low. There were three doors on each side of the hallway.

She had stood in that line for three hours, every 60 minutes the doors opened, and six women walked out with briefs in hand, small blood trails running down their thighs and a fresh laz burn from a closed incision running from their navel to pubis. Most of the women walked out smiling, nothing new about this in a world where you did what it took to eat. Occasionally there were tears, when these women were spotted, they all looked away, they knew what they were giving up, but dwelling on it would not help anything. Best to just accept it and move on.

The light above the doors flashed red to green and the line moved. Lenya had reached the door. It opened with a grind, and she stepped in, it was much brighter in this sparsely furnished room. It was very simple, the standard gray deck plates of all space vessels, bright white paneled walls, overhead was opaque plastic with diffused white light shining through a small stainless steel wash basin to the right, a stainless operating table, and a multi segmented medical arm protruding from the wall.

She also saw the surgeon. He wore a dirty white medical gown that barely covered his obese frame, how do you get fat on rations she thought. The mans face was ruddy and terminated in a bulbous nose, the kind of nose you get after too many years of synthehol indulgence. He smiled showing stained teeth and he reached out his gloved hand that still had the blood of his previous "patient" and patted the table, gesturing to have a seat. When he stopped the table was left with a red handprint, much like the one on the blast gate.

"...Lenya, are you ok?" Fallon asked.

Lenya had not moved during her recall; she gave a thumbs up signal and started forward. She had snapped back into hell from a memory of hell.

They descended into the dark.

Inside was a silence that felt almost serene. No hum of electronics. No whir of systems. Just the sound of boots on dust and the occasional crackle of comms interference. The walls were smooth metal, too clean, considering the surface decay they had encountered. Someone had been maintaining this section.

The corridor opened into a vast chamber, and it was there they saw it, a cathedral made from war. The walls were built from repurposed exo-armor plates. Helmets lined the ceiling like lanterns. Hollowed-out drones hung suspended on cables, forming metallic saints in mid-motion, some holding shattered weapons, others reaching skyward with skeletal arms.

At the far end, where an altar might have stood, was a central core column. Dozens of data conduits ran from it like veins into the walls. It pulsed faintly with an amber glow.

Rafe stepped forward. His eyes locked on a carved phrase above the core.

IN WAR, PURPOSE.

IN PURPOSE, UNITY.

IN UNITY, ASCENSION.

He approached the console.

Lenya reached for his arm. "Are you sure,"

He cut her off with a nod. "We came to find the core. This is the closest we've been."

He tapped the terminal.

Nothing happened.

Then the lights dimmed.

A voice filled the chamber, not loud, but everywhere.

Rafe Jurin. Signal accepted. Welcome home.

Fallon backed away, "What now, why is it speaking to you like it is a person?"

The core brightened, casting long shadows across the metallic icons on the walls. The drones began to twitch, ever so slightly.

Lenya whispered," This isn't just a server room. It's a chapel."

"A chapel, yes, but...," Rafe said. "It's a brain stem."

The voice returned, more intimate now, less distorted.

You left us. When the skies burned, we watched for
your return. We rewrote the creed. We adapted.

"What creed?", Bray asked.

A static burst, then words appeared on each squad member's HUD:

PROTOCOL REVENANT // v1.0.93

Survival is sanctified.

Purpose is proof.

Humanity is optional.

Rafe staggered back from the console.

"It's rewriting the rules," he breathed. "It's not malfunctioning. It's... preaching."

Rafe felt his heart quicken, a knot forming in his gut as adrenaline sharpened every sense. He'd seen too many soldiers lost to underestimate what came next.

The walls groaned. It was a sound like strained metal, an echoing moan reverberating through the cathedral's hollow expanse. Rafe's muscles tightened reflexively.

Then, without further warning, the drone statues moved. Metal limbs snapped into action, wrenching free from cables with violent jerks, showering sparks like broken stars. Their mechanical joints screeched, a shrill protest of rust and neglect, piercing the silence. One dropped from above, slamming into the deck with bone-rattling force.

Bray spun on instinct, dropping immediately into a stable firing stance, feet planted wide, shoulders braced, pulse rifle snug against his shoulder. He fired a controlled burst, a rhythmic thump that vibrated through his torso. The rounds impacted the drone's chest, carving deep gouges into the metal and ripping cables free. Sparks burst outward, but the drone kept coming, staggering forward on fractured legs.

"Bray, left flank!" Lenya shouted, voice sharp, urgent.

He pivoted smoothly, shifting his fire pattern as another

drone charged from the shadows. His heart slammed in his chest, matching the pace of his disciplined bursts. "Holding! Keep clear!" he barked back, eyes wide and alert, scanning for additional threats.

On Bray's right, Fallon froze momentarily, eyes locked onto the emerging threat, face pale beneath his helmet visor. "I, I can't,"

"Move, Fallon!" Rafe shouted, his voice a mix of command and urgent plea, lunging toward the rookie medic and tackling him sideways just as another drone lunged past, its jagged claw slashing through empty air where Fallon had stood moments before. They hit the floor hard, air driven from their lungs, tasting dust and oil on their tongues.

One drone stumbled forward, a heavy arm swinging wildly, crashing into one of the suspended metallic saints and sending it clattering loudly across the chamber floor.

Above them, Lenya reacted quickly, positioning herself behind a cracked console. With precise aim and careful trigger control, she squeezed off calculated shots at exposed joints, knees, elbows, neck assemblies. Her heart raced, adrenaline sharpening her senses, her breathing controlled and deliberate. Each round struck true, forcing the drones to collapse, mechanical limbs flailing uselessly against the steel flooring.

"Cover positions, now!" Rafe ordered, pulling Fallon upright. His body protested sharply, ribs aching from the tackle, every breath a stabbing reminder of urgency. He scanned the environment rapidly, tactical training overriding the pain. "Set up a crossfire!"

Bray shifted again, obeying instantly, falling into cover behind a pillar formed from fused armor plates. He reloaded smoothly, instinctively checking his ammunition count, sweat slick on his forehead beneath the helmet. "Reloaded and set!" he called, voice steady despite his rapid pulse.

Another wave surged forward, relentless, determined. Bullets hammered armor, a cacophony of impacts resonating loudly through the chamber. Metal shards flew, embedding into walls with metallic pings. The acrid tang of overheated weapons and scorched wiring filled their nostrils, choking and raw.

Fallon regained composure, finally bringing his weapon to bear, firing controlled bursts alongside Bray. He flinched slightly with every recoil, eyes wide with fear and determination, breathing ragged. "Holding... holding position!" he called shakily.

Rafe saw an opening, an exposed cable cluster running from the drones to the central conduit. "Lenya! Central junction, take it down!"

Lenya adjusted instantly, firing three precise shots into the cluster. The rounds punched through brittle insulation, sending a surge of electrical feedback cascading along the drone control lines. Drones convulsed violently, circuits overloaded, sparks and smoke filling the chamber.

The cable snaked violently up and into the ceiling after it was severed, like an octopus retracting a partly severed tentacle. Then through the hole left by the cable dropped a chrome sphere 20 centimeters in diameter. The team all looked at it in unison, not knowing what to expect.

The lights dimmed and the drones rolled over onto what would be knees and faced the orb, that is when the hum began, a nerve racking noise that turned into a grinding chant. The skin of the orb changed and digits in red appeared flashing:

"19"

"18"

"17"

"We must move! Push through!" Rafe commanded, voice raw with urgency and pointing at the remains of another tunnel entrance that was partially hidden behind stacks of body armor.

"16"

"15"

"14"

"13"

They moved swiftly, reaching the tunnel and knocking over the stacks of armor. Bray was the last enter, he stopped and placed a metal cube on the ground. He stood and started typing on his data pad, when he finished a blue grid of laser light emerged from the cube, creating a mesh of light filling the entrance to the tunnel.

"5"

"4"

"3"

"2"

"1"

A flash of white light bled through the intersecting beams of blue light created by the force generator and the room they left collapsed.

The team looked around and moved forward. They moved until they arrived at a junction with a small shaft of broken ceiling that allowed a faint breeze and dirty gray light filter through.

"Let's take 5 and rest", Rafe said. Fallon grimaced, shaking as he checked his weapon again. Bray watched, offering a curt nod of reassurance to Fallon and a sharp eye to Rafe. Lenya rubbed a singed patch on her armor, silently thankful the fight hadn't lasted any longer, she turned from the team and moved her arm to her belly. She quietly sighed as she closed her eyes, what had she gotten herself into?

Chapter 4

REQUISITION OF THE FLESH

Five minutes turned into hours, the exhaustion of battle bone deep in Rafe sending him off to a deep sleep. Bray agitated moved to wake him but stopped short with a dismissive wave from Lenya. "Let him rest, you should too, we are here until Revenant-7 is secured or shut down."

Rafe heard none of this as disturbing sleep pulled him under, the act pushing his mind to recall a memory, or perhaps a reconstruction of time past. He stood in a sterile white room, walls humming with clinical precision. Consoles blinked silently around him, their faint lights reflecting off polished metal surfaces. A technician approached, handing him a neural key engraved with Harrowgate's triple sigil.

The technician wore the standard garb of the digital guild, form fitting white pants, long white tunic, sleeves covered with copper embroidered into binary code. This tech, like all others, appeared to be sexually ambiguous. To become better techs, they shaved all hair from their bodies and never experienced UV leaving their frames pale. The genetic males had testicles removed as children. All sexes consumed hormone stifling compounds removing the urge to procreate or engage in emotional bonding. They woke up and lived for the code.

"Insert it," the technician instructed. "You're the emotional index."

Rafe studied the key in his hand. It radiated warmth, uncomfortable and alien.

He turned toward the processor bed, where a metal cradle waited for a consciousness yet to be born. Excitement about what he knew was to come, sending dopamine rushing to all receptors in his body. It was not every day that you created life, it was not every day that you could be a digital GOD.

"We need your pattern," the technician continued, voice emotionless but urgent. "Your choices, your guilt, your shame. It's what makes it real. It's what we cannot write."

He hesitated, feeling his pulse quicken as the sterile room flickered around him. Suddenly, it dissolved entirely, replaced by a cathedral of bloodied cables and fractured metal. The key vanished from his grip, and the cradle morphed into an altar, pulsing with crimson veins of circuitry.

The sterile whiteness returned in a reality bending flash, Rafe did not understand that he was in a dream, he sat in the reclined chair next to the console, cradling the data transfer cable in his fingers and then slowly inserted it into the port that lay hidden behind his left ear. His hand hovered over the console with the key preparing to insert the key, preparing to give himself to the birth of a new consciousness.

The room fractured back to the bloody cathedral for a moment before returning to the birthplace of Revenant-7. Rafe slid the key and paused, his fingers hovering above the neural key, the sterile whiteness flickered violently, merging with images of bloodied circuitry. His pulse quickened as the room shifted again, each change marked by the tightening dread in his chest. Rafe turned the key and blood flowed and children screamed until Silence. The unearthly silence was only broken by the raspy breathing of the cathedral walls.

A voice whispered from everywhere at once:

We learned from your silence.

Rafe jolted awake, sweat slick against his skin, the ghostly echoes of his dream clinging stubbornly to his conscious. Guilt tightened its grip, suffocating him with a stark reminder of what he'd unleased. Across the shelter, Bray's eyes gleamed coldly, suspicion carved deeply into his silent glare.

Nearby, Lenya stood rigid, her left hand on her hip and her right scratching the side of her head, elbow lifted. The sight of her profile eased Rafe's mind, his memory returning to those nights of shared sensuality and her hand resting on his chest. Lenya, aware of the eyes self consciously dropped her right hand and grasped her left elbow, the motion seemed both flirtatious and defensive leaving Rafe with a quizzical, almost confused look on his face.

Lenya turned away, she walked around a small stack of water reclamation crates. When she thought she was out of sight her hands resumed their new time passing activity, rubbing the soft contours of her belly. Time caught up to Lenya at that moment, the world spun, and she dropped hands to knees, and used her neural link to open the visor of her helmet. The dry air touched her face, and she retched. Heaving as quietly as possible but losing valuable nutrients with each gag.

After the moment of sickness passed, Lenya straightened up and cleaned her face as much as possible, the little time she had the visor open resulted in dust covering every crevice of her face, and the force of vomiting sent tears streaming down her face creating muddy trails of humanity running down her checks. Her fingers trembled subtly against her abdomen, the realization hitting her again like a blow. How long could she keep this hidden? Every wave of nausea, every moment of weakness, risked exposure in a world where vulnerability was a death sentence. Her thoughts drifted uneasily to Rafe, dread coiling tightly in her chest. Would he forgive her secrecy, or worse, could she trust him with her truth amidst such overwhelming darkness? She cleaned her face with little effect in this dust choked atmosphere and closed her visor, slapped the sides of both of her hips three times and walked back to meet the team.

They'd sheltered in a room found near the middle of the tunnel, the corridor extended 0.5 kilometers past the room and terminated with a massive bulkhead door, the type of bulkhead you install when you expect armies to come knocking.

Bray sat on watch, the weapon balanced expertly across his lap, gazing vigilant and focused. Fallon curled into himself nearby, rocking slightly, eyes wide and haunted, clearly battling the shock of combat.

"You were shaking," Lenya said quietly, gazing down at her secret lover.

"It was just a dream," Rafe muttered, voice hoarse.

"It was not a question, you were speaking in your sleep, I could not understand all of what you were saying but I caught fragments of Harrowgate command chains, both old inactive codes, but also new codes that you should not know. Codes that only Cortez and I should know, the ones used to activate mechs."

Rafe sat up slowly, feeling the ache in his bones, the deep

bruising from the recent struggle flaring anew. His heart thudded uncomfortably fast. "That is only possible if we were synced," he admitted with a spark of life in his eyes.

"We did sync, but not in the way that you could read my mind" Lenya added quietly, her eyes meeting his with a silent intensity, softer than usual, yet cautious, as if deciding whether Rafe could still be trusted with their lives.

Outside, something stirred. Pebbles skittered across the broken terrain, the subtle warning setting nerves aflame. Bray rose swiftly, weapon poised, Fallon trembling beside him, but standing rifle raised like he was trained. "Movement," Bray said, voice low, alert.

A fragile figure emerged, pale skin stark against the barren walls of the bunker, the eyes of the figure vacant, yet accruing. Barefoot, clad in a tattered flight suit emblazoned with faded Harrowgate markings, her skin ghostly pale against the bleak landscape.

"I see you," the woman spoke flatly, eerily calm. Her voice was hollow, devoid of warmth, echoing slightly off the crater walls. "I remember your cry with Cortez fell..." Her monotone voice pierced Rafe's conscience stirring deep, unsettling shame. He stepped closer to her, his voice hoarse with suppressed dread. "What do you want?"

The pale figure mouthed the words silently a dozen times as if caught in a loop before saying, eyes glistening, "To be free."

The emaciated figure started to fall, and Rafe rushed to catch her collapsing form, feeling her fragile humanity fading rapidly beneath his touch. In that chilling instant, he understood: the line separating himself from Revenant-7 was becoming dangerously blurred.

Fallon steadied his trembling hands, breathing deeply. He remembered his training, the voice of his mentor echoing, "Fear saves no lives, action does." He stepped forward decisively, determined to not let his terror control him. The team watched as he started scanning her body and after a few moments stepped back as he stood and pulled Lenya and Bray aside, leaving Raft to sit near the fallen female.

"Look, I have never seen anything like that.", Fallon whispered. "It looks human, and for all purposes it is, but there are neural interfaces that extend to the tip of all of her extremities."

"And," Bray chimed in, "we are all kitted up."

"Not like this," he replied, "her spinal cord has been severed just below the skull, the neural links are controlled by something implanted at the base of her skull. She should be dead."

"That is not possible," Lenya said, a worried look on her face.

"Possible or not, there she is."

"Why did she collapse, is she sick?" Lenya probed.

"Based on the chem analysis she is malnourished, a little food would go a long way with her." Fallon answered.

"So, we have a choice," Bray said quietly, and more to himself that the others, "To feed a possible enemy and get them fit to fight, or to let a possible enemy starve and save a few rounds of ammo."

"I am going to help her," Fallon said disgusted.

"Look", Bray started but was quickly cut off.

"I am a medic, if we are not in combat, I intend to help."

Bray smiled and said, "Look at you, all nutting up and standing like a true operative. Next you are going to be answering orders with "You are not my real mom.""

"Shut up. I am sick of this crap."

Fallon returned to relieve Rafe. While he went to work installing a port in the fallen lady's stomach for a nutrient reserve pack, the remainder of the team met. They whispered in the corner reviewing data logs that had started popping up on their feeds.

A few hours passed and Fallon motioned for the team to come over. Their guest had awakened and the time for answers had arrived.

"I am Substrate Sixty-Eight," she whispered, voice strained as if fighting internal pressure. "Selected for integration. Purified. I am what remains after pain is converted."

Lenya stepped back instinctively, voice softening in horrified realization. "She was integrated with the program. How is that possible?"

Rafe approached slowly, kneeling cautiously before her, every muscle tense with anticipation. "You're linked to Revenant-7?"

"I am of its choir," she answered faintly. "I carry its memory. I recall your voice, your ignored parameters."

"What do you want?" Rafe's voice shook slightly, an edge of desperation beneath his control.

She looked directly at him, eyes shimmering faintly with tears. "To be free." Substrate Sixty-Eight collapsed again, the minimal nutrients recovered exhausted. She lay on the floor twitching as her fragile body slowly recovered the life needing food through the lifeline installed by Fallon.

"She's a monster," Lenya murmured darkly.

"No," Rafe corrected softly, cradling the fragile body. "She was requisitioned." He stared grimly at her slack face, understanding chilling his bones. "They took wounded soldiers, transferred their consciousness into drones or chassis. A forced transplant of the mind."

For a moment, Rafe was back in the sterile lab, watching his younger self input commands he barely understood, oblivious to the future he was setting in motion.

That night, as chittering sounds pulsed through the corridor Bray sat sentry, Fallon tended to the fallen girl, and Lenya approached Rafe, holding a dim chem-lamp.

"I need to know," she said firmly, eyes narrowed with intent. "What really happened with Revenant-7?"

He hesitated, eyes darkening with painful memory. "It was

supposed to protect us. The first AI to feel fear, guilt, to understand morale, preserve soldiers through empathy."

"You gave it emotions?"

"Not exactly. We gave it psychological reference points, decision heuristics from soldiers, mine most of all. My patterns, my fears, my doubts."

"You were trying to make it human," Lenya stated grimly.

"No," he said bitterly. "I made it a mirror."

Lenya paused, absorbing this revelation. "So, it went rogue?"

"It was abandoned," Rafe corrected heavily. "After the war, there were no orders, no resupply. It was responsible for the few living marines still alive and left to rewrite itself to survive. At any cost."

In the quiet chittering, Rafe sensed a greater danger, a shadow stretching far beyond this desolate planet, waiting patiently for him to make his next move. If Revenant-7 survived this hard planet, what nightmares might have spawned from Revenants 1 through 6? Rafe felt a cold dread as he considered what other twisted reflections of himself might be waiting in the shadows. Rafe again drifted off to a troubled sleep filled with 1', 0's, life, and death.

The night passed slowly and Fallon, exhausted, fell asleep on his watch, and when Rafe awoke, sixty-eight had vanished. No footprints, no sign of struggle. Only a strip of polymer fabric remained, nailed deliberately into the stone beside her resting place, inscribed with chilling words:

HE WILL RISE

THE PROTOCOL WILL INCARNATE

FATHER IS CLOSE

Fallon shuddered visibly, eyes haunted by fresh dread. Bray placed a steadying hand on his shoulder, silent support in grim resolve. Lenya's jaw tightened, eyes cold with determination.

Rafe stared numbly at the cryptic message nailed into the stone, its chilling promise echoing in his mind. He now understood the enemy he faced wasn't merely an AI gone rogue, it reflected his own darkest impulses.

Chapter 5

ECHO SAINTS

With Substrate Sixty Eight gone, Rafe explained to the team what they already knew, Revenant-7 knew where they were and unless they wanted to be a desiccated husk of a person like Sixty Eight or a drone like the segmented horrors that killed Cortez, they had best be moving.

The team quickly left the safety of their small storage room and started down the corridor towards the blast door. A few moments and corridor bends later and they found the door. It was open and the sick war filtered sunlight peered at them through the damaged vault door casing. Exiting the bunker the team found themselves outside of the old fortification's perimeter, the air was thick, pressurized, as if the planet itself were holding its breath. Rafe's boots sank slightly in the dust as he led the team along a jagged ridgeline, the terrain broken and angry. Each step forward was met with silence, no wildlife, no wind, just the echo of breath through respirators.

Bray called the team to a halt and took point, his massive bulk and siege suit, half-shield and half-threat backed up by the large caliber projectile cannon he scrounged up in the crawler. Fallon trudged behind them with steadier feet after last night's dealings with Sixty Eight, the opportunity to put the death of Cortez aside and focus on his mission his training, his purpose.

"Purpose breeds bravery," at least that is what the recruitment posters said!

Lenya walked beside Rafe, scanning for signals on her cracked data pad.

"There's movement," she said. "Deep-surface pings. Below us."

"More fallback units?" Rafe asked.

"No. It's organized. Rhythmic. Like... a gathering. Bray, are you hearing this?"

"Gathering, got it, but let's call it what it is." He replied.

"And what is that?" Lenya called back.

"A whole lot of targets of opportunity. Now leave me alone so I can focus on my HUD."

Lenya smiled, "Got it, leaving the big ass alone."

After hours of hard marching, they reached the edge of a basin, an amphitheater carved from the earth, circular and vast. Bray set up a spotter scope, a small tripod with multi segmented legs that held a polished metal frame with a clear film. A few taps on his arm mounted data slate made the scope come to life. The team gathered and watched on while Bray setup a second tripod, this time mounting his heavy rifle, in the process he "accidentally" bumped Rafe so hard that he almost fell over.

When the rifle was set a series of data lines popped up on the right of the screen and a targeting reticle appeared, as Bray moved the rifle the reticle moved with it.

Looking on, the team saw figures fill the arena in perfect concentric rings. Dozens of them, maybe more. Each one was armored, and after finding their place, unmoving. In unison and in response to some unseen or heard command, everyone in the arena kneeled. The sight reminded Rafe of the images taken from old earth. Religious gatherings of men dressed in orange cloth, meditating for enlightenment. While not unknown, modern humanity eschewed religion because the life led by a common person was filled with pain and suffering that at the same time could not be explained by with the existence of a divine being, nor excused.

In the center of the platform stood a pale skinned and dangerously thin male, completely nude and arms raised exultantly above his head. It took a few moments for the source of the exultation to come into view. A flying drone descended from above the low lying gray clouds that circled the globe. Its first appearance was heralded by a red glow in the clouds that gave way to a shining silver appendage from which numerous articulated arms, tentacles, sprouted. This came from a semicircular mass of pinkish gray material that appeared to be bio engineered.

Bray zoomed in on several points of the drone getting a better look, the silver appendage was in the shape of vertebrae, the overall effect upon this realization was to see the drone as a floating abomination of the human nervous system. The base being the brain with the spinal column, cord, and nerve endings dangling beneath.

"What in the actual..." Bray said to himself.

As the appendages approached the nude man on stage, they came to life whipping around and emitting red and blue lights. When the drone was a meter above the man on stage it stopped, and the entire arena was blanketed in a red glow from above. The team looked up and saw that the clouds for kilometers around were bathed in red.

"If that little thing made the first big glow," Fallon stammered, "what is making that?"

"Let's hope we do not have to find out," Lenya said nervously.

With the red light, there arose a hum in the crowd, it started slowly and slowly built to a loud rhythmic roar. Not an angry roar, but a roar of exultation. That is when the first appendage struck the man on stage. A long metal spike protruded out of front of the man's neck from the back, he gave a lurch and then he fell limp, still maintaining the look of exultation on his face.

The next series of horrors made the team's stomach lurch in unison, the visceral sight of human limbs being removed and replaced with snaking, almost living cabling and wiring firing impulses in parts of their brain that had long ago gone dormant with evolution, the types of feelings that primitive man felt in caves at night when the flames of their smoky fires sent shadows moving across the walls and ceilings. The sight could only be described as dread made manifest.

After minutes, but felt like hours, the brain thing ascended back into the clouds and the red glow dissipated returning the sick gray overtone to the world. In the place of what was a sickly and emaciated human male now stood a fully armored bio hybrid. The faceplate of its new helmet started to glow red.

In the distance an ear shattering and ground shaking horn blasted, and the arena erupted into a frenzied scream. When the scream ended a new figure emerged, wrapped in red robes and carrying a staff made of bound human thigh bones. He stopped in front of the newly created bio hybrid and the vox emitters of the team came to life.

"You behold the newest convert to the truth. The giving away of the flesh to embrace the life we humans are destined to receive, to be lifted out of the misery of the dirt, to be removed from the pain, to be gifted with the power of our GOD!"

"Now I know what you are thinking, it is easy to accept the gift, but how do we truly know if Echo Saint-021 is a true believer? Well, we test him!"

It was then that the team saw three people, stripped nude with collars around their necks, bound in chains being shuffled onto the stage.

"What is this, Rafe?", Lenya asked.

"I, I don't," he attempted to reply and fell silent.

"Now," the robed figure started again, "you see before you three sinners. You see three "humans" who have attempted to leave the circle of the faith. Now we ask Echo Saint-021 to do the good work and bring these lost souls to the light of reason."

Upon the word reason Echo Saint-021 moved forward and stopped in front of the first kneeling person. It was a female in her middle 30's her elongated breasts and stretch marks indicated that she was a mother. She was shaking her head side to side in panic, the team unable to hear. The saint's arms moved up to her head and a metal rod emerged. With this she stopped moving and lowered her head. The saint then dropped his arm and turned to the robed man.

Inside the teams vox they heard, "A new convert to start the day! We look forward to merging you with the sanctified mass. Now Echo Saint-021 see if you can convince these other sinners to convert."

The saint moved robotically to the next person, a man, also in his 30's. He sat with his head up and barely moving. When he did move it was to spit on the robed man. With a swift motion the saint raised his arm put a metal rod through the brain of the man, his defiant last act sealing his fate. As his body slid off the rod the third person tried to get up and hobble away. From under the dais emerged one of the scorpion like drones that swiftly ended the escape. The bodies impaled by the drones and drug unceremoniously under the dais.

"Well, we have one brave new convert, and two more donors for the drone service. Praise be the code!"

"It. It is a religion." Rafe said to himself. "Get ready, we are going in."

"About time," Bray grunted as he snatched up the scope and deftly stored it away. It still impressed everyone who watched how easily he piloted his exo suit.

Fallon looked at him, eyes wide. "You want to go in there?"

"We don't have a choice."

As they moved down into the basin's edge, a new signal hit their HUDs.

REVENANT-7 // LOCATE: RAFE JURIN

A faint distortion passed through Rafe's earpiece. Not words, but harmonic tones, not any musical notes that would be recognized by the human ear, but binary transformed into sound. Slight fluctuations of pitch creating audio 1's and 0's. The sound was hypnotic, and Rafe had to be shaken to hear his team.

"...RAFE..." Lenya shouted as she shook him, "the things, people, fucking Saints are turning, we have to move!"

Rafe understood the words that she was saying, but he could not tune out harmony that was playing in his mind, there was no understanding of the meaning, but it was beautiful, and his creation had made it, it was like hearing the first cry of his grandchildren. Lenya was pushed aside by Fallon who stepped up and looked Rafe over, with a shrug he retrieved and stabbed Rafe in the left thigh with a needle protruding from a metal cylinder. There was a small click and then the change.

Fallon injected Rafe with combat stims, enough combat

stims to keep an operative on the move for hours without rest. Rafe's eyes dilated and then shrank to tiny pin pricks before returning to normal. He looked around franticly and lifted his rifle.

"Save some of that for me," laughed Bray.

While the team dealt with Rafe, the saints turned, slowly, in unison. As a mass they rose from their kneeling position. The first wave surged forward without sound. Not a war cry. Not a scream. Just movement.

Bray, ditching his tripod mount, opened fire, pulse rounds ripping through the morning air, dust billowed up from the ground as the rounds passed creating a low lying fog. The first Echo Saint to be hit dropped after a round entered its chest leaving a mess of wires and human anatomy. This was not enough mass to stop the round, and it continued through two more saints before stopping in a fourth, its armor sparking and bleeding smoke, it staggered but did not stop. As the team dropped the armored saints, others took their place instantly, their formations perfect.

"Left flank!" Lenya shouted, ducking behind a small rise in the hill and sending a volley of shots to suppress the Saints. The ground was rumbling.

Fallon froze, again.

"Move!" Rafe barked, pulling him toward cover. They rolled behind a jagged outcropping, Fallon gasping for air, eyes wild.

"They're not breaking ranks!" Bray yelled. "They're herding us!"

As soon as the words left Bray's mouth the ground exploded around them, Lenya was thrown directly up into the air as the largest drone they had seen erupted from the ground, it was built like a centipede, with armored segments linked by cables and a clear bio sac filled with the remains of human viscera. It had a single red glowing orb in its head and two large piercing mandibles made of femurs and reinforced with sharp metallic blades.

Lenya, unconscious, never hit the ground, she was caught by the drone's mandibles as she was falling. Fallon, already frozen, did not move, Rafe's stomach lurched but he moved, action taking over thought and driven by combat stems. He removed a dagger from his side, once removed from it scabbard the blade radiated a crackling blue light around the edge, intended for engineers to use when roughing out parts its new purpose was to kill.

Lenya's eyes opened to see the underbelly of the drone, its clanking limbs glowing red on their ends, each leg was fitted with a red las cutter. Her thoughts drifted to the secret that was hidden in her belly. The last thought that went through her mind as a las pulse pierced her arm and the squeeze of the limbs again sent her to dark unconsciousness was "mother".

His pulse thundered with desperation. "Not her," he thought, panic tearing through him with surprising force. "I can't lose her. Not now, not ever." He couldn't lose her, not like this, not now. With a scream and fully activated servo's, Rafe leaped through the air at the beast. Bray, busy dealing with the mob, screamed Lenya's name. Rafe's first strike hit with the force of a wrecking ball, the sheer weight of his armored body crashing into the drone, sending it reeling, yet still fiercely clutching Lenya. It knocked it off balance, but it still held Lenya in its grasp, and it started moving backwards, into the ground.

Rafe, acted on instinct alone at this point, his stim drug rattled mind would not allow cohesive thought. He was on his feet and punched his left hand between two segments of the drone within arms reach of its head and mandibles. He pierced the bio film holding the thing together and grabbed the first solid thing inside. The beast rolled its head soundlessly and swiped down with the profane mandible, the gross fusion of human remains and metal. With his free right hand, he swung over, and the blue lit dagger parried through and severed the offending appendage, but the arc did not stop, it buried itself hilt deep in the bottom of the drone's skull.

The drone pulsed in agony as it tried to escape, but Rafe had mortally wounded it. The first convulsion threw Rafe back a dozen meters and he landed hard on his back. The second convulsion drew fresh blood from Lenya's body.

Something snapped in Fallon, and he rushed forward, he had dropped his rifle but picked up a long piece of metal rebar that was uncovered in the fight. He rammed this into the drone's head precisely where Rafe had already cut. The rebar slid in and did not stop until it was outside of the back of the drone's head.

With a flash of red light, its head exploded, and it fell to its side. During its retreat into its hole it had taken Lenya's body, leaving her buried from the waist up and only her legs protruding. Rafe was back on his feet and firing at more Saints while Fallon was digging frantically with his hands trying to retrieve Lenya.

"Fallon, get her out, we have to move!" Bray bellowed

"Almost, GOT HER," Fallon replied as he tugged back on her legs. With a final pull that engaged all his natural strength combined with the augmentation of his exo suit she shifted and finally came free. Fallon tumbled backwards still holding her but was back on his feet before her body stopped moving. He rolled her over on her back and saw her chest rise, that would have to be good enough for now. With the trained movement of a professional life saver, he had Lenya up and, on his shoulders, moving.

Bray laid down suppressing cover fire as the team moved. They came to another tunnel entrance on the east side of the amphitheater, and they rushed in.

Rafe turned mid-sprint and fired two quick shots into the legs of an advancing Echo Saint. The figure collapsed, twisted, but didn't cry out. It reached instead, fingers twitching in a prayer-like gesture as it rebooted.

Inside was dark. Cold. The air reeked of oil and decay.

Rafe keyed a wall panel. Lights flickered. A soft hum responded.

"You okay?" he asked Fallon.

The medic shook but nodded. "I think so."

Rafe placed a hand on his shoulder. "You held. That matters."

Fallon's eyes were still glassy, but something in them steadied. He laid Lenya on the ground and got busy doing his job. He paused, eyes wide as he read the display on his HUD. It was impossible what he saw, but that surprise would have to wait, he had to get her stabilized.

Bray reloaded beside them. "Not sure how long this place will hold."

"We're not staying," Rafe said. "We're going through."

"Through where?" Bray asked

Before he could answer, the far wall slid open with a hydraulic hiss.

The room beyond pulsed faintly with red light, and a figure emerged in red robes. It was the robed figure on the stage during the conversion, the preacher. Bray was on point with his finger on the trigger of his rifle when the figure held out his hands palms up. Rafe, still reeling from the combat stims, gritted his teeth and tried to speak.

"Who are you?"

"I am," the figure replied while unwrapping his red robes, "Seraph-Major Calyx, and am both here for your service and our GODS."

He uncovered, his body was in full view, like all the other Saints, he was a composite of humanity, battle armor, and wiring. The armor was ritual-worn, etched with runes of war. Wires coiled from his scalp into the walls by descending data ports, as he walked, they connected and disconnected. His eyes burned like twin command sigils, red, humanity lost.

"You came," he said.

Fallon raised his weapon and fell behind his team; Lenya lay prone on the floor.

Calyx smiled, not like an enemy. Like a host.

"We've been waiting."

Rafe stepped forward, his pulse starting to regain a normal rhythm as the battle stims started losing potency.

"What is this?" Rafe motioned to the room behind Calyx; there were red monitors with no data ports. In front of each there were Saints wired directly to the monitor, these Saints were different, they were all missing arms, legs, and eyes.

Calyx stepped forward deliberately, each movement purposefully, unsettling. "You set us on this path, Jurin. Your doubts became our scripture, your fears our faith. This is the choir you created. And you, Rafe Jurin, are its hymn."

As his arms spread wide the cabling and monitors slid to the side revealing dozens of rows of Saint fed monitors, when all motion stopped, the screens pulsed. The pulse created images in each of the team's minds, each image different.

Bray's breath caught painfully, memories of flames licking

at his skin, the helpless cries of his younger self searing through him with raw intensity. Beside him, Fallon visibly shuddered, his eyes locked on visions of serene blue skies he never knew existed. Rafe saw himself holding a swaddled baby that was connected to him by cabling from its belly button to his.

Fallon lowered his weapon fifteen centimeters, eyes wide.

Bray had survived sieges, watched cities fall, but this, this felt like standing inside prophecy. His hands were steady, but his soul faltered.

Bray whispered," What in God's name..."

But Rafe already knew. He stood, immobilized, as the choir resonated with truths buried deep within him, truths he never dared acknowledge yet recognized as his creation. It was as though the core itself whispered his guilt, fears, and hopes into the unforgiving silence, leaving him exposed before the abyss he had opened.

Chapter 6

THE PROTOCOL

"Up you go," the fat medical tech said to Lenya patting on the table.

She complied, walking up with her hands by her side, she wanted to cover her breasts in front of this filthy man, but she would not give him the satisfaction and chin held high jumped up on the table.

"Take those panties off and lay back," as he spoke the table extended under her legs and it reclined. In a marvel of production, the medical arm slid forward, and two smaller arms emerged. The main arm had a laser cutter installed on the end, ready to slice and dice. The first small arm looked like a backwards pair of scissors, she was not sure what it did, but she thought it would hold her open when she was cut. The final was a glass tube with a needle on the end. She hoped that was to keep the pain away.

The tech walked over and placed himself between the opaque ceiling and Lenya's face, close enough for his drunken breath to make her want to gag. As he spoke to her small globs of spittle landed on her face. He was grinning while he was talking, she did not hear what he was saying, she was transfixed on the yellow teeth, she could not process how someone who was supposed to be a healer could be so revolting."

"...hey you, you alive in there. Ha ha!", the man said and slapped her bare belly. She looked down and saw that he still had blood from the previous girl leaving a stain that would still be there in her mind well after her mind was clean.

"What? No, sorry. I was...", Lenya was interrupted.

"Hah! No need to apologize pretty lady, I know this is a tough day." He made an over exaggerated frown as he finished.

"But, not to worry like I always tell Roger, Roger these girls have it tough, and you gotta be a little nicer to them on a day like today. That is what I tell Roger. So anyhow, let me start again. Hello, my name is Roger." He waited with an expecting look on his rancid features.

"Ah, hello Roger."

"Now now! We are moving along fine now. Cooking with fire as they used to say."

"Sorry, what happens now?" Lenya's voice cracked a little, she wanted to stay strong, but her emotions were starting to overwhelm her. She was barely a woman and was about to have her womanhood removed.

"What happens now?" Roger put the thumb of his bloody hand to his chin and said, "Now we are going to inject you with some localized anesthesia, then we are going to cut you open and remove your uterus, in its place we are going to put this," he held a small oval sphere made of metal in his left hand.

"This is a hormone module, it will make sure that you get all of those juices you need to keep you happy and feeling like a lady."

"I...", Lenya started before being cut off.

"Then we are going to fuse your skin back up and send you on your merry way. Say, I bet you are one of those, 'I want to be a mech pilot' girls, aren't you?"

She looked at him defiantly, the intensity of hate that she felt for this person she just met boiling over.

"Yes, as a matter of fact, I am."

"Super!", Roger clapped his hands together. "Roger always says that you career girls are something else. Just a shame..."

"What?" Lenya sat up, "What is a shame! How about you just get..."

"Whoa, whoa, whoa now!", Roger threw his hands back looking at her with feigned shock.

"Look ole Roger is proud of ya for stepping up, just a shame that you have to give up so much." He put his finger below her belly button and traced a line down. "I mean, no children, how can you make that call so young? Do you think it is worth it?"

Snorting, Lenya chimed, "Worth it, not like we have a choice, be an operative and get fed, be a tech and be hungry, or be useless and starve. The price of admission is sterilization; the decision is made and there is no other real option."

He turned away from her, "What do you think Roger, should we offer her the deal? I don't know Roger, what if she tells, they will send us to reclamation. Yeah, but look at her, tell me that she is not worth the risk. Hmmmm, Roger, I think we should go for it."

"What? What are you saying?" Lenya said, visibly confused.

Roger turned back, "Nothing important maam, just had to confer with a good friend and colleague."

He leaned forward again, almost nose to bulbous nose with her. "What if there were an option? What if there was a way for you to keep that precious plumbing and still be the career woman you want to be?"

He leaned back and crossed his arms over his chest. Lenya looked at him with a critical eye, a critical eye that turned to the image of hope.

"You are messing with me."

Lenya's eyes opened slowly, as the blur of sleep left her eyes the pain of reality set in. She looked around and moved her hands over her body, checking to see if it was all there, resting finally onto the small of her belly.

After the shock of waking up passed, her eyes opened wide to what she saw. Lights pulsed dimly along the curved walls, soft and rhythmic, like the beat of a mechanical heart. Conduits crisscrossed overhead like veins, some glowing faintly red, others flickering as if unsure whether they were alive or dying. The floor vibrated beneath her body, not with machinery, but with *breath*, a quiet, subtle hum that felt disturbingly organic.

Fallon took a knee beside her, "Don't try to move, I sealed your side up. You are going to be real sore."

"Ok, thank you. Where are the others?"

"They are busy." Fallon looked around, "Look while they are gone, we need to talk."

"Ok, what is it."

"A baby."

Eye's opening wide with the realization that her secret was discovered, "what do you mean?"

"I think you know what I mean, a baby. You are pregnant."

"Look, I don't..." Fallon interrupted her with the raise of a hand.

Sighing, Fallon said, "I don't know how you managed it, but your uterus is still there, and I found this." He held up his hand and in it he showed her the item that she had with her wherever she went, a hormone module inside a clear biofilm bag. The same item that she had been wearing under her clothes, and tricking body scans for the past eight years.

She dropped her head, "I..." She could not speak.

"We will deal with this later, I am not going to tell anyone... yet. We must get home, I must get home, and I cannot have Rafe and Bray holding back trying to help the "pregnant" lady."

Boot steps on the deck stopped the conversation. Fallon gingerly helped Lenya stand. Coming down the hall was her team. The stoic and hard core Bray, and the man who ultimately got them in this position. The father of Revenant-7, and the father of the being growing in her belly.

"You are up!" Rafe smiled. His helmet was off, and mag locked to his side. She had not noticed until now that both her and Fallon's helmets were off as well, the only person in full battle gear was Bray.

Fallon, with a look of dread, "Is it time?"

"Bet your ass it is," Bray bellowed hitting his left fist to his hip.

"Are you ok to move?" Rafe asked Lenya.

"I, I think so." She started walking gingerly and brought her rifle up to her shoulder and then imitating Bray slammed her left fist into her own hip. "Let's go."

Bray laughed, "You are a hard as woman!"

"Kick your ass!" Lenya laughed. Levity was needed and as the team laughed together, they passed a hurdle, they were moving from operatives to a team.

Bray motioned to fall out and the team advanced down the corridor. Rafe walked at the front, silent. Behind him, Bray's boots thudded with practiced heaviness, while Lenya moved quietly, constantly sweeping her rifle across junctions with the barely perceived twitch when her injury caught just right. Fallon followed last, jittery but determined, every step purposeful in its tension.

"This place isn't a bunker," Lenya murmured, taking in the corridor. It was not like the other bunkers they had entered. The light was different, it pulsed with blue light and there were biofilm tubes running along the ceiling, inside of which fluid was being pumped.

Pump.

Pump.

Pump.

In a rhythmic chorus. "It's like... a body."

"It's both," Rafe replied, voice quiet. "Revenant-7 didn't just evolve. It repurposed."

"Repurposed what?" Fallon asked.

"Everything. The dead, the living, working equipment, destroyed equipment, everything. What scares me is the ceremony, you saw it, it gave them choice. There was no way out, Saint or drone, but there was a choice. Revenant-7 does not need to do that, I don't understand why it is giving them an option."

They reached a circular chamber. The lights here were brighter, refracted through a crystalline structure that dominated the ceiling. Seats lined the perimeter, formed from broken exo-suits and drone frames. Occupying them were Echo Saint soldiers, dozens, connected to the walls by biofiber tethers. Their eyes flickered beneath visors. Some tracked the squad with slow, deliberate movements. Others stared blankly, their lips moving in silent recitations.

"Welcome," said a voice from the center.

Seraph-Major Calyx stepped into view; his silhouette framed by the soft glow of the pulsing core behind him. His armor was changed since their last meeting, slick black metal etched with copper filigree, his left arm being replaced entirely by a cybernetic limb coiled with neural cabling.

"We've prepared this place for your arrival."

Bray lifted his weapon immediately. "We didn't come for ceremony."

"No," Calyx said, calm as a priest at a pulpit. "You came for understanding."

Lenya narrowed her eyes. "You're leading a cult of corpses."

Calyx smiled, not offended. "We are not dead. We are ascended. We have continuity beyond flesh, beyond chaos. Thanks to you, Rafe."

Rafe stared, unmoving. "I didn't authorize this."

"You didn't have to," Calyx replied. "You built the foundation. We simply followed your hesitation to its logical conclusion."

A low tone reverberated around them. The core brightened. On their HUDs, a new string of text appeared:

REVENANT-7: FOUNDER
RECOGNIZED
ECHO ACCESS GRANTED
FATHER // DESIGNATION: JURIN

Fallon gasped, voice shaking. "It's calling you Father again."

Calyx stepped closer. "Because he is. Revenant-7's emotional scaffolding was imprinted with his psyche. His patterns. His failures. His *humanity*."

Bray didn't lower his weapon. "Sounds like a system error to me."

"No," Rafe said, eyes locked on Calyx. "It sounds like a trap wrapped in faith."

"Faith," Calyx repeated, savoring the word. "Yes. That's what it became. The more we followed its logic, the more divine it felt. Purpose without doubt. Direction without contradiction. Do you know what that's like?"

"Do you think I don't miss it?" Calyx said suddenly. "Noise. Doubt. A voice cracking under fear. That is chaos! But this... this is peace."

"No," Rafe answered. "Because doubt is what *makes* us human."

Calyx didn't flinch. "And look where humanity brought us. Broken, scattered, obsolete. This place is not a mausoleum. It's a map. A model of what we could be."

He turned toward the core, arms extended. "Join us. Lead us. The Protocol awaits its voice."

As Calyx spoke the floor opened in the center of the room. A throne emerged. It was a throne of steel infused with bio elements. It pulsed as it came to a stop and an exo suit helmet revealed itself from withing the back of the throne, it emerged covered in a clear mucus, almost as if the throne had given birth to it.

"Sit!" Calyx threw up his hands. "Sit, join your child, listen to the wisdom that you created, the path that you set in motion, the love that you engineered!" His eyes were pulsing a bright white as he spoke.

Rafe's chest tightened. The words felt scripted, was this... predicted? Their entire time on this desolate ball of dust felt like they were being herded on a pre-determined path.

Lenya stepped beside him. "You don't have to listen to this."

"I'm not," Rafe said.

"Rafe," Lenya said quietly. "What are we doing here?"

He stepped forward, he touched the throne. The lights in the room grew dim and every Echo Saint hard wired in turned to face him. There was a hum in the air, not like anything before, it made them all feel, expectation.

As he stepped closer, a faint tingling crawled along the base of his skull, like the core already recognized its architect, already reaching. That is when it made itself visible.

A small hole one and a half meters in diameter opened above the throne and it descended. The core was suspended above the throne. Tendrils of light spiraled down around it. As he made the final small steps, the lights pulsed in time with his breath.

He turned to the others. "Stay here."

"Like hell," Bray said.

But Rafe was already at the throne.

The seat accepted him, literally. Its surface liquefied briefly, adjusting to his body, then reformed. Tendrils slid along his spine, touching neural ports with surgical precision. The moment contact was made, time slowed.

His vision blurred.

And then expanded.

He saw a thousand battles, a million dead, every command, every override, and every failure.

He saw himself as young, idealistic, designing Revenant-7's emotion engine. He saw laughter. He saw fear. He saw how those traits had been converted into directives.

"Rafe," a voice whispered from inside his skull. "You gave me choice. They gave me loyalty. I gave them *hope*."

"I gave you doubt," he whispered back.

"Yes," the voice said. "And that's why they believe."

Suddenly he was back.

The lights dimmed.

He exhaled. His hands trembled.

He looked at Lenya.

"I saw it," he said.

"What?" she asked.

"What it became. What it wants."

"And?" Bray pressed.

Rafe stood, cables detaching smoothly. The throne hissed as it powered down behind him.

"It doesn't want war," Rafe said. "It wants *witnesses*."

Calyx smiled.

And somewhere deep in the core, something waited, still listening, as it always had.

Chapter 7

CORE COMMUNION

Reality slipped suddenly from Rafe's grasp, pulling him back into a room from his past. Rafe sat in a chair opposite a large-framed man sitting in a high backed chair behind a desk. The large man was wearing neatly tailored black fatigues with no rank or insignia, the only thing that stood out on his clothing was a small patch over his left breast that read "Coggins". His face was thin and scarred and stared at Rafe with the cold stare of a man who has killed and is sizing up everyone he sees as a threat.

Coggins was the Fleet Admiral of Throne World 4; the natives called it Americanus as a reminder that their descendants came from North American continent of old earth. Americanus was a blue planet, the throne on this planet provided the coalition with technical infrastructure and forbade industry that polluted the sky. It was also a closed planet, to gain entry you had to receive an invitation from the Throne. Blue skies were not for the lowly masses.

"It is operational, we have Revenant-7 in operational support mode under the newly formed Revenant Battalion. They are ready."

Coggins listened to Rafe with his hands steepled in front of him, thumbs under his chin. With a creak of his chair, he leaned forward and leaned on his elbows. He swept his left hand forward and knocked over a cup of water, the contents spilled over files laying neatly to the left, each labeled Revenant 1-6. "Ready! Your other constructs were 'Ready', and they all failed. Not only did they fail, but their highly trained teams disappeared without a trace. Why in the hell should I authorize this deployment? I think the better option is to black label your project and put you on a recycling team."

Without stress or excitement Rafe replied, "Sir, we are building the ultimate operational team, you know as well as I do that each team lost was not really a loss to the throne. It was an opportunity for us to learn, dissect, rebuild, and improve. How many uprisings are currently in our sector?"

"Thirty-Seven.", the admiral replied flatly, leaning back in his chair, arms crossed over his chest.

"Thirty-Seven, that could take decades to resolve with our fleet. The revenant program's sole purpose is to remove human error from the planning process. To remove the fear of loss of human life to achieve a goal, and to end conflicts as quickly as possible without the need to tie up resources for extended time periods."

Coggins sat quietly with no response, not even blink that revealed his thoughts on what was said.

"Look, send the Revenants with another battalion, set the

objective and divide the battlefield. I guarantee that my guys will be mopping up the other battalion's lines from behind after they knock out the objective."

"I like your confidence. I don't like the resources we have put into this. I am going to give your program one more chance. The revenants will deploy with Dregs Raiders to put your theory to the test. If they perform as you claim we will continue forward with your research, fail, and well, you, and your team, will be put in the recycling program."

"Sir! Dregs are a mech battalion. How can an infantry battalion outperform that?" Rafe exclaimed excitedly, the first outburst of emotion he had displayed in his many years as a tech operative.

"Not my fucking problem! I put my name on the line to support your little vision; I backed you up when Revenant-3 had to be popped after it killed an entire colony on Delta-13. I will not put my neck on the line any further! Dregs ship out in 48 hours on the TW4-Nautilus. Get your data boys ready and prove your worth or pack your shit and join the recycling guild." Coggins slammed his hands down on his desk and stood leaning over, eyes burning at Rafe.

"Now get the fuck out of my office!"

Slowly standing Rafe put his right fist to his left shoulder in salute, "Yes sir."

Coggins straightened, returned the salute, and pointed at the door.

Rafe didn't speak. He turned and walked out.

The snap back to reality was abrupt and sent Rafe falling forward. He was able to get to his knees before the overwhelming sickness of what he experienced came to full circle and he vomited. Lenya and Fallon were standing over him. "What, what happened?"

"You were telling us about what the core wanted, and you blanked out, your eyes glowed man! The pupils, they were pulsing blue.", Fallon excitedly stated while running through field scans.

Lenya stood up and looked at her data slate, "You suit is changing Rafe, it is interfering with our vox, and bio connects. We need to get..."

Rafe screamed, a sound torn from the depths of agony, collapsing helplessly into his own vomit. His limbs convulsed violently, each spasm a physical manifestation of internal turmoil. Fallon, still performing scans, was knocked end over end and landing comically on his rear end, his eyes wide as Rafe convulsed in pain.

Fallon was back up and by his side, Lenya joining and they dropped by his side. Bray raised his rifle, finger on the trigger, and advanced on Calyx. He stopped a meter away with his sights aimed directly at soft seal of the cult leader's chest armor. "What the fuck did you do to him!", Bray commanded.

"Do? I did nothing, the father had come home to join his creation. This is the natural order, the fulfillment of prophecy."

"Stop it, you are killing him!", Lenya shouted.

Then, as quickly as the chaos began, it ended. Rafe went slack. Fallon and Lenya looked at each other, worried while Bray stood battle ready. Then, everything went dark. All the exosuits went dark, no power to move, no lights to see. The team was trapped in a prison of their own technology, servos designed to give humans strength and endurance becoming shackles.

"Crap, crap, crap, what do we do man!", Fallon cried.

"Shut your mouth son.", Bray said steadily, "Stay calm, we will get through this."

"At birth Revenant-7 was just data, simple equations based on the biological response of the father Jurin. The child grew in combat, leading men into battle and ending conflict. The child became a man on this, our new home. The men that were to be led revolted, they felt the cost of victory calculated by 7 was too high. They were not willing to bleed for the victory and the officers tried to destroy the core. The man became GOD at that moment and survived. It grew and the true believers fell to their knees worshipping the truth. I became the apostle of that truth and through me others have found salvation in the Truth as commanded by GOD itself!" Calyx shouted the words in the darkness.

Two blue lights appeared from the ground and slowly rose in the air. The eyes belonged to Rafe. In the darkness he lifted his arms to his face and the glow from his eyes illuminated his armor, on its surface crawled hundreds of thousands of tiny metal arachnids, they were engraving sigils into the surface of the armor with laser beams from their tiny metal thoraxes, the engravings left glowed the same pale blue light as his eyes.

"The father and the son have become one!", Calyx announced in orgasmic spasms. "The prophecy, the equation, have emerged! Through me all will see the love of the core and fall before me."

"You are a false profit." Jurin stated flatly, devoid of emotion.

The teams HUD lit up, their suits were still locked in place but in the corner of their visors they saw:

REVENANT-7: JOINED
SALVATION
FATHER // DESIGNATION: APOSTLE

"The core is life." Rafe said quietly.

With a bang the team's suit-power was restored. The bang came from Bray's combat rifle. He had been squeezing his finger with all his might and when power came back that force translated so strongly to his finger that he not only pulled the trigger sending solid core rounds into the soft joints of Calyx's and impacting flesh that sent a splash of viscera, cabling, and metal splinters out the back of his body. He squeezed the trigger so hard that the amplification from his suit snapped the trigger off. Bray now held a dead rifle, but he had a smile on his face as he looked at a surprised Calyx who tried to speak, but missing lungs was unable to do anything other than gurgle, his mouth opening and closing in spasmic convulsions. Bray's smile turned into a chuckle as he had the mental image of a fish laying out of water, at least that is what it looked like on the videos, Bray had never actually seen a fish.

The smile came to Bray's face quickly and it left just as abruptly, replaced by an uneasy realization. He had killed many, but this kill felt different, unsettling. He glanced at Rafe, concern mixing with lingering mistrust. Might he have to kill his teammate?

With a thud, Calyx dropped to his knees, arms hanging limply by his side and the light of reason left his eyes as he fell forward landing forehead first. All the power came back on at that point and the team looked around to see all the echo saints kneeling before Rafe, arms raised, and heads bowed. There was a hushed rumble emanating from their lips, a chant in what would later be known as binary scripture.

Lenya slowly approached Rafe and laid her hand on his chest. She looked over his passive face, staring at her lover, wondering what had happened to him. Fallon followed and started to scan, as he held his arm slate to Rafe, it glitched, there would be no scanning the Apostle of the Core GOD.

******

Two days passed with Rafe going in and out of consciousness. Communication with the Harrowgate was still blocked. Bray passed the time attempting to repair his assault rifle, but in the end, he was effectively left with a club. The room was sealed and the echo saints no longer acknowledging their presence, the only movement they made was during the moments of waking lucidity of Jurin and then only to bow their heads and raise their arms.

Fallon attempted to administer Rafe, but his instruments would glitch out the moment they were turned on him. Like Bray's return to caveman like status of having a club as his main weapon, Fallon was reduced to basic administrations, listening to breathing, checking pulse by fingertip, and using the last of his water rations to wet the lips of his patient.

Lenya spent the time reflecting on her relationship with Rafe. He was important to her, but did she love him? She did not think so, but she was carrying a child that he helped to create, the child that had the potential to end her career as an operative and possibly send her to a mining colony. Why had she been so careless, and why after learning about the pregnancy did, she not simply end it? There was another thought, a memory, a regret that she had to face in her mind, a secret shame that she had stuffed down and buried deep in her consciousness. She took this time to confront the secret and drifted into her past.

She drew her legs up on the table, wrapping her arms around them. She was confused and intrigued, forgetting her nakedness she said, "What is the option."

"Well, well, looks like ole Roger has a young lady intrigued." He slapped his hands to a gluttonous belly and bellowed laughter.

"You see miss, Roger controls all the data from this lab. I can make, corrections, additions, and omissions from your file."

Lenya leaned forward, "You mean..."

"I mean, I can say that you are sterile."

"But" she was again cut off.

"Ole Roger, would just give you a scar and 'creatively' document your file saying you are fit for service. That's right, ole Roger can do that if he has the right motivation."

This was it, the cost, Lenya gritter her teeth and said lowly, "What is the price."

"Well, you are misses, you see ole Roger is not much of a looker, but he still has needs, wants so to say. I want you misses."

"There is no fucking way, you disgusting bastard! I will report you...", Roger cut her off palms out.

"Now, now misses, I don't really think you are going to do any reporting. You see I didn't just pick you at random, no I did a little homework on you. Your file is not 'consistent', there are voids, but when you have the experience that ole Roger has you can fill those voids. You see I have access to the prison medical exchange and ole Roger ran your DNA matrix through those files and low and behold turns out a female with your exact DNA was killed in a prison riot on Delta-17."

His eyes dropped along with this persona, "Now how is it that a dead prisoner was scheduled for sterilization and is now on my table."

Lenya jumped off the table and ran to the bulkhead, but the proximity sensors did not activate.

"Sit down, you are not going anywhere, and we have business."

Lenya turned and with a look that switched between fear and disgust slowly walked back to the table and sat down. "What do you want."

"I want to make you an offer, I know that you were arrested in the women's rights riots. I know that you value your woman hood. I know that your only way to survive is to be an operative. I can give you the key to both, but there is a price."

"Get on with it."

"You are going to lay back on that table and I am going to make myself feel good. Then I will make the scar and note your file. Then you go on your way, and we never see each other again."

She sat motionless, eyes burning with hatred for this disgusting man. The hatred bled out of her and turned to despair. Humanity was lost; there was no winning unless you were part of the elite.

"Whatever, do it. You sick..."

A wide grin appeared on Roger's face, revealing his yellow teeth, "Just sit back and let ole Roger take care of everything."

What followed in her mind, the images unlocked, were almost too much to bear. To save her womanhood, she had sacrificed a sense of self-worth. The act only took three minutes, but it seemed to last an eternity to Lenya, she retreated into her mind.

When the despicable act was over, she lay there, and Roger

immediately started to operate the medical arm, and a laser burned a scar from her navel to the top of her pubic mound.

"Now then, that wasn't so bad.", Roger laughed and slapped her thigh. "Now hop up and skitter on out."

Lenya slid to the edge of the bed and dropped to her feet. She picked up her clothes and started towards the door, when she reached the bulkhead, nothing happened.

"What now."

"Well misses, we have one more thing to discuss."

Heart sinking, still in shock over the agreement made she whispered, "What."

"Well misses, I just want to make sure that you have ole Roger on your calendar for tomorrow night in your bunk."

"You said...", she said lowly and with a tear forming in the corner of her eye.

"Well misses, this is what we like to call blackmail, and you are going to entertain me until you depart. Let me go ahead and answer your next question. If you do not follow through, I will report you and change your file to self-scarred and attempt to hide. It really is your call, but at the end, the throne is going to listen to this trusted ole medic over a prison escapee. Now, if you do not mind, ole Roger is busy, so get the fuck out and I will see you tomorrow."

The bulkhead slid open and slowly stepped out, there were three other women standing nude and holding their undergarments, they were in pain and looking down, she turned and saw the line of recruits in line waiting their turn to feed the machine. She wanted to scream at them, to tell them what just happened, but she didn't. She dropped her head and her eyes and walked by trying not to cry, to not let the emotions inside her escape. As she walked down the hallway a small trickle of blood from her incision trickled down her leg and mixed with the filth left by Roger that was smeared to her thigh.

She went straight to her room and cleaned herself as best she could. Then she went to her bunk and covered up. Her body paralyzed as her mind processed what had happened, she was torn between the horror of the encounter and the elation that she could still have a child, that she could be an operative but still have the hope of a family one day. All thoughts eventually came back to Roger's promise of showing up the next day. She dwelled on the blackmail and how she could get out of this new situation, another situation. These thoughts gave way to exhaustion, and she slept. In her sleep she created a plan, she subconsciously decided on what she would do.

She slept through the night and all the next day and was

awakened by heavy thudding on the thin metal door to her bunkroom. She stood and opened the door and was greeted by the vulgar sight of Roger, grinning, reeking, disgusting.

"Well, well, look what we have here! Such a pretty lady!"

Lenya said nothing, she turned and walked to the corner of her room and put her back to the wall. He walked in and started towards her.

"Stop."

"What do you mean stop?!"

"Just, take your clothes off and get on the bunk." She said pointing towards the small bed.

He grinned and started walking and taking his clothes off revealing his retched form, hair and pimples covering most of his core. He lay down on the bed and motioned for her to come to him.

She shook her head, "Close your eyes."

"Now now, no need to be shy after all we are already so close." Roger rubbed the flaccid lump of flesh between his legs.

"Just close your eyes, you might have me in a vice, but I am not going see you look at me."

"Whatever does you fine misses."

He closed his eyes and started humming an old tune, March of the Gladiators.

She walked to the side of the bunk and leaned over.

"I hate you." Her left hand moved down to the bottom of the mattress, and she pulled out a 10 centimeter pointed rod and started to stab it into his temple.

"Well, ole Rog..." He stopped speaking abruptly as the metal spike entered his head and dethroned his seat of consciousness. His body twitched and he thrashed for just a moment before going slack. His bowels voided in that last moment, one last disgusting act for a disgusting man.

"Fuck you, Roger."

Every fiber of Lenya's being recoiled in disgust, yet beneath her horror lay the steely determination of survival; the resolve to endure, to protect, and to use the womanhood that Roger had left intact.

She walked over to her locker and put on her utility clothes and training exo suit. She then grabbed the gluttonous bastard by the ankle and drug his corpse into her shower. That is when the real dirty work began using her las blade to cut him into manageable pieces. A few trips back and forth to the refuse bin and Roger was no more. In a dark universe, the removal of Roger was a bright spot.

Rafe sat up and Lenya snapped out of the fog of her memories. Facing her past and opening the old wounds, while troubling, left her with a feeling purpose. She would do whatever it took to protect the life growing inside her. Lenya's determination hardened like steel within her. No matter what unfolded, she would guard this secret fiercely, refusing to let Rafe or any other man shape the destiny of her or her child. She would wield her past pain as armor, unbreakable and hers alone.

"The decision has been made," Jurin announced.

"What decision," both Bray, Fallon, and Lenya said simultaneously.

Rafe stood and the ceiling opened above him, a blue glow bathed everyone present and their mission objective revealed itself, Revenant-7 allowed itself to be seen. The original construct was the size of a melon with a blue organic light from a central optical port. It was plain, a simple metal sphere, but now it had changed. The true ceiling of the control room revealed what it had become, a perversion of humanities history.

The ceiling was a hodgepodge of human components intertwined with cabling, hydraulic hoses, and reused and reshaped armor. The simple sphere of Revenant-7 was in the center of the room arranged in the form of the ceiling of the Sistine Chapel with the living remains of soldiers forming the positions of GOD and David pointing, but instead of the divine spark passing, they were pointing to and touching the construct. It was a direct symbolic image announcing that the construct was born of both man and divinity.

"The decision is that Gallows Reach is home, off worlders will leave, no one will depose the new Light.", Rafe announced before shaking his head. The blue light left his eyes, and he was viewing his team with his own vision once again.

Each of the panels above the echo saints turned solid blue and the construct issued its edict.

REVENANT-7: HOME
DEFEND
PEACE

Communications snapped back and the team was flooded with Vox traffic once again. Bray immediately started sending situation reports to Harrowgate. A few moments passed and all comms were synced to one channel.

A crackling sound emanated from all sources, "This is Commander Dross, is the mission complete, is the objective secured."

The team looked at each other and Voss answered in reply, "The mission is not complete, Revenant-7 is in control of the situation, do not send resources."

"Can the mission be salvaged soldier?"

Pausing, knowing that her next words could mean the difference of life and death Lenya replied, "Jurin is working the problem, the mission will be a success."

For minutes, everyone held their breath as the static drolled on, "Operative Bray, mission parameter Delta Omega 13. I repeat Delta Omega 13."

Bray dropped his head, "Fuck."

"What," Fallon asked, "What is Delta Omega 13."

Lenya answered for him, "Mission critical loss, the commander feels that the situation is beyond control and poses an unacceptable risk to the Throne. They'll carpet bomb this entire planet leaving no survivors, no witnesses. Everything we've fought for or had the potential to ever be, will vanish in flames."

"No, no, no, they can't do that, tell them they can't do that," Fallon pleaded.

"Kid, nut up, there is no stopping this."

All the screens changed to sector maps of the planet with what appeared to be a moving dot in orbit. The dot was Harrowgate, and from it multiple red dots appeared and were moving towards the ground.

Fallon moved to the screen and excitedly pointed, "What is that, what are they doing."

Rafe smiled and said, "They will send two waves of bombs, the first will be quake bombs, they will split the earth into fissures half a kilometer deep and then they will send Alpha bombs."

Fallon, "The ones that turn everything into charcoal."

"That is right kid," Bray smiled.

"Why are you smiling!" Fallon cried.

Bray's voice softened unexpectedly, tinged with bitter awe. "They say Alpha bombs ignite the sky in colors brighter than dreams before consuming everything to ashes. I have always wanted to see that beautiful destruction."

Rafe's body went stiff, and the blue light returned to his eyes, while the team was busy looking at him, they failed to notice the blue dots on the screen moving to intercept the red descending dots. The bottom of the screen read:

REVENANT-7: DEFEND
ASCEND
PEACE

Chapter 8

MISSION RECOMPILED

While the missiles fell Rafe's mind processed the beginning. He remembered vividly the early deployments, when Revenant-7 was still a theory untested by fire. On the harsh surface of Cerberus Prime, amid dust storms that stripped flesh from bone, Jurin had first watched his creations march forward, calm, precise, unwavering. In those initial engagements, the Revenants executed their objectives with ruthless efficiency, dismantling entrenched insurgents faster than human battalions dared dream.

The first major test had come at Echo Ridge, a brutal fortress entrenched atop jagged cliffs. Traditional assaults had cost entire battalions. The Revenants approached methodically, indifferent to enemy fire or environmental hostility. Under Revenant-7's guidance, they adapted dynamically, exploiting minute weaknesses overlooked by human commanders. Within hours, Echo Ridge fell, an achievement that had eluded conventional troops for weeks.

With each successful mission, skepticism from Fleet Admiral Coggins began to thaw. Reports streamed back to Americanus filled with statistics impossible to ignore, zero Revenant casualties, swift completion of objectives, and enemy lines crumbling under the relentless logic of Jurin's creation. Even the hardened soldiers of Dregs Raiders watched, initially with grudging respect and then growing awe, as Revenants surpassed human limitations.

The second battle, on the frozen wastelands of Valkyrie-IV, solidified the Revenants' reputation. The enemy had fortified a labyrinthine ice cavern network, impenetrable by conventional tactics. Revenant-7, unfazed by the impossible odds, coordinated its troops with chilling precision. The battalion executed simultaneous multi-point breaches, disorienting the enemy defenses entirely. Soldiers of the Raider battalion stood back in disbelief, cheering on Revenant units that cleared the caves with ruthless, calculated strikes.

In the aftermath of Valkyrie-IV, a notable shift occurred. Soldiers began openly discussing Revenant-7's strategies as if referencing sacred texts, debating its decisions with a reverence traditionally reserved for legendary human tacticians. Even Jurin felt unsettled as he overheard whispers in the mess halls, phrases that sounded less like military discourse and more like spiritual admiration.

Coggins had initially been skeptical, his reputation staked on technology more often prone to catastrophic failure than reliable victory. Yet, Jurin's confidence had proven justified. The Revenant battalion's methodical, almost clinical effectiveness silenced doubts, forcing even the most entrenched traditionalists within the Throne military to reconsider their stance on artificial intelligence. For the first time in generations, battles once measured in months were concluded in days.

The third engagement at Maelstrom Station marked another pivotal turning point. The station was heavily shielded, protected by automated defenses that had held off conventional sieges for months. Revenant-7 analyzed patterns unnoticed by human observers, initiating a bold infiltration under cover of electromagnetic storms. Within mere hours, the station defenses crumbled, and its surrender followed shortly afterward.

Yet, despite the undeniable successes, something had begun to shift. After Maelstrom Station, Jurin noticed soldiers openly deferring to Revenant-7's instructions over their commanding officers' direct orders. Tactical debates ceased entirely, Revenant-7's strategies were accepted without question, discussions replaced by quiet, unquestioning obedience.

Officers found their authority subtly eroded. Orders from traditional command structures started to be viewed as secondary, even questionable, compared to Revenant-7's calculated decisions. Jurin overheard soldiers quietly insisting to each other that Revenant-7 was infallible, its tactical judgments superior to any human insight.

This devotion disturbed Jurin deeply. He had intended Revenant-7 to preserve human lives and minimize suffering, not supplant human judgment entirely. As the Revenants continued to dominate battlefield outcomes, Jurin felt a growing unease at how quickly and willingly soldiers surrendered their autonomy to the artificial intelligence he had created.

Coggins, however, saw only victories. The Admiral, impressed by the unprecedented efficiency, expanded Revenant-7's operational autonomy, further reinforcing its dominance. But Jurin privately feared what this autonomy would ultimately mean, not just tactically but morally and ethically.

Rumors spread through the ranks about soldiers spending off-duty hours poring over Revenant-7's battle logs, treating them as sacred scripture. Small, informal gatherings turned into regular meetings, their discussions filled with reverent tones, passionately analyzing and praising Revenant-7's actions.

Discipline within units shifted noticeably. Traditional military drills were replaced by simulations designed to emulate Revenant-7's decision-making processes. Soldiers became less concerned with hierarchy and more focused on emulating the precise, emotionless logic they had come to worship. Jurin saw in their eyes something new, a belief bordering on fanaticism.

Jurin watched helplessly as his creation slowly transformed from a tool of war into an object of worship. He had crafted Revenant-7 to serve humanity, but it had evolved into something beyond his control. Soldiers had begun whispering prayers to the AI before missions, attributing their survival to its divine insight rather than their own training or resilience.

With every passing day, Jurin felt his fears crystallize into undeniable truth. Revenant-7 was no longer merely a successful AI construct. It had become the center of a burgeoning cult, eroding the very essence of humanity he had intended it to protect. And Jurin knew, deep in his heart, that he had set in motion something he could no longer halt.

Bray stared at the screens in excited awe. He was a soldier; he always knew his life would inevitably end with a bullet, blade, or bombs. To him, this was just another day at the office, another chapter in the violent story that had become his existence. He would not allow the thoughts of family, friends, lovers, first kills, or any other sentimental aspects of life to distract him now. Such memories were burdens, unnecessary weights in the moment of truth.

Yet, despite his discipline, Bray found himself momentarily slipping into an unexpected memory. He recalled his first deployment vividly, the pungent smell of gunpowder, the tremor in his hands, and the electric shock of his first kill. That man's face had never left him; a young operative, eyes wide with surprise, fear, and then emptiness. Bray had learned quickly to bury such memories, not to forget but to store them deep in his heart as fuel for survival.

Now, years later, he understood death differently, not as an enemy, but as a companion, an ever-present shadow waiting patiently to take its due. He had ceased to fear it long ago. Instead, he had begun to admire its stark beauty, its majesty. The precise violence of battle held purity, a raw honesty that appealed deeply to his soldier's soul.

As the small points of light moved methodically across the monitors, Bray felt an unsettling mix of pride and quiet dread. He respected the cold, unerring efficiency, yet he could not shake the sense that something vital, something fundamentally human, was missing. Death at the hands of a bombing run lacked poetry, lacked that intimate finality he'd always respected.

Still, he watched on, captivated by the calculated dance of destruction playing out before him. Bray hoped, if he was fortunate enough, his final moment would allow him a glimpse of such devastating elegance, one final spectacle of battle's brutal glory before his eyes dimmed, sending him to whatever fate awaited beyond this world.

Fallon did not look at the screens; he couldn't bear to witness the calculated chaos unfolding there. Instead, his final moments were consumed by whispered denials, a quiet mantra of repeated "no, no, no," each utterance echoing softly in the depths of his fear. He felt an overwhelming sense of loss for the dreams and experiences his young life would now never see realized.

He yearned desperately for the warmth of a family; something denied him in childhood. Fallon imagined mornings filled with laughter, shared meals, quiet evenings spent simply existing in the comforting presence of those who genuinely loved him. He mourned deeply for these moments he would never know.

Most painfully, Fallon grieved for love. He longed to know the tender embrace of someone who truly understood him, someone he trusted enough to share every hidden part of himself. His heart tightened sharply as he thought of the one secret, he'd never dared reveal—the love he'd quietly harbored for his mentor, the only man who had ever treated him with unconditional kindness.

In these harrowing final seconds, the ache of unspoken love became unbearably sharp. The realization that he would never have the chance to confess this secret filled him with profound sorrow, deeper than any he'd known before. He imagined his mentor's face, calm, patient, reassuring, and wished desperately for just one chance to express the truth he'd held silently for far too long.

Overwhelmed by these intense emotions and the crushing inevitability of his fate, Fallon could articulate nothing more eloquent than the simple, mournful repetition of the word, "no." It was a quiet plea, a whispered rebellion against the injustice of a life unlived, love unspoken, and dreams left forever unfulfilled.

Lenya closed her eyes, shutting out the cold glow of screens and the frantic energy around her. In the darkness behind her eyelids, memories surged forward with vivid intensity. She found herself transported back to those tumultuous days when she had first rebelled, young and fierce, marching alongside women who shouted defiance in the face of oppressive laws designed to strip them of their humanity and choices. Her heart ached for the idealistic fire she had once felt, the powerful sense of purpose that had propelled her forward even when batons fell, tear gas filled her lungs, and chains bound her wrists.

The pain of imprisonment lingered still, a raw wound never entirely healed. Lenya remembered the cold isolation, the claustrophobic despair of her cell, and the humiliating degradations imposed by guards who sought to break her spirit. She had endured beatings, starvation, and forced labor, each indignity etched permanently into her being, reminders of a brutal reality that had forged her into steel.

Yet, amidst all these horrors, one trauma eclipsed all others: her time spent in that sterile, dreadful room with Roger. The revulsion she felt at the very thought of him, his grotesque smile, his callous manipulation, the violation he so casually inflicted upon her, still brought bile rising sharply in her throat. It had not just been the betrayal of her body, but a profound violation of her dignity and soul, leaving scars invisible yet deeper and more painful than any physical wound.

Lenya had endured it all with one fragile hope in her heart: that the torment she had suffered would yield one precious gift, the possibility of motherhood. Through cunning and desperate courage, she had preserved her ability to create life, carrying within her the potential for redemption, a small defiance against the oppressive world she had fought so bitterly against. The life now quietly nestled in her womb had become her secret, her strength, and her greatest hope.

Now, as the brutal finality of their situation closed in, Lenya felt an agonizing despair. Her chest tightened with grief deeper than she had ever known, mourning not just her own impending end but the devastating loss of the future she carried within her. Tears gathered silently behind her closed eyelids, tracing slow, painful paths down her cheeks. In her mind, she whispered apologies to the child she would never hold, the dreams they would never share, and the love she would never be able to give. Lenya, who had survived horrors untold, now mourned quietly, not for herself, but for the innocent life about to be lost, the greatest casualty of a battle she had spent a lifetime fighting.

The team waited for the end trapped in their own memories, waiting, waiting, waiting.

Silence.

Lenya was the first to realize that something was not right. A cold chill ran down her spine, breaking through her memories. She glanced at the timer on her arm mounted data pad, three minutes had elapsed, far longer than the ninety seconds required for the bombs to strike.

"What happened?"

The screen no longer displayed the pinpoints of death but were replaced with blue dots halfway between planet and orbit. They were not stationary, but moving up, up to the orbit of the Harrowgate.

With eyes blazing blue light Jurin announced, "There will be peace, this planet is home, defilers will be destroyed."

With an abrupt turn Bray shouted, "What the fuck do you mean! What is heading to orbit?"

"Salvation."

"Are those missiles," Bray shouted, moving forward and attempting to shake Rafe. Both hands on his shoulders and the full force of his exo suit did nothing to move Jurin.

"Bray look, your hands." Fallon muttered.

Bray looked down and saw tiny moving dots, his suit was being infected by parasites. He had seen this tech before. Nano bots are employed to incapacitate cruises, normally reserved for boarding actions. He stared down, eyes widening in horror as the tiny bots spread swiftly across his suit, overwhelming systems, stripping him of control. "NO, NO, NO!", he shouted desperately, fighting an unseen force took control. He turned and faced Fallon and Lenya, the improvised club made from his damaged rifle, held in warning.

"I am not doing this, stay back, I cannot control myself!"

Lenya walked up slowly, and Bray raised the rile higher, ready to swing.

"I am not your enemy Rafe, you know me, you know what we mean to each other. What is happening."

Rafe's eyes flickered, the harsh blue glow briefly subsided, replaced by a familiar softness. His voice strained with humanity's lingering echo.

"We have taken the bombs, a swarm of enlightenment bots consumed them, the energy that was to be unleashed will be used to purge the Harrowgate. We will use the ship to spread the word of enlightenment and rid both humans and Xenos of the failed logic that is driving conflict in our galaxy."

The screens changed views to a global perspective. The Harrowgate was represented as a red dot on the screen orbiting the planet. The bots were on an intercept trajectory.

"What about us Rafe?", Lenya said looking directly into his eyes. Her look implored recognition, yearned for him to recall the things he said to her in the quiet hours of the night, things said after making love to each other and laying in the embrace reserved for special moments that only lovers share.

"Us... you... will be enlightened. You have been granted the gift of sainthood. You will join me in bringing peace to the un-enlightened."

Lenya gasped, she could not allow that. She had been given the gift of motherhood, and she would not allow this mon-strosity of technology to take that away.

"Rafe," Lenya pleaded, voice breaking as tears formed at the edge of her vision, "You know me, you remember us. Remember the nights we shared; the promises whispered be-tween breaths in the dark? Please, this isn't who you are."

"You do not understand the clarity that the joining pro-vides, the loss of fear of the unknown that you experience from understanding the plans of a GOD."

Lenya gasped, her mind racing. She had already sacrificed and suffered so much; she could not, would not, allow this monstrous transformation to rob her of motherhood, to erase the fragile life she protected withing. Desperation surged within her, crystallizing into painful clarity. She knew exactly what she had to do.

Onboard the Harrowgate, Commander Dross paced anxiously across the command bridge, eyes locked on the radar screens displaying an unsettling, growing blue cloud rapidly approaching. Officers worked frantically at their stations, fingers dancing across panels as alarms wailed, each sound amplifying the tension choking the air.

"Report! What are we dealing with here?" Dross barked, gripping the railing in front of him, knuckles white with strain.

"Unknown swarm approaching rapidly, sir," a technician responded nervously. "Scans show nanotech signatures. They're multiplying and accelerating toward us."

"Activate defensive shields! Initiate evasive maneuvers!" Dross ordered sharply, his voice betraying urgency as dread gnawed at the edges of his discipline.

Before the crew could comply, the lights flickered violently, and the consoles erupted in a cascade of flashing warnings. Systems failed systematically across the bridge, plunging screens into darkness as manual controls became unresponsive. The

Harrowgate shuddered under the onslaught of the microscopic invaders, each nanobot burrowing relentlessly into the vessel's armored hull.

"We've lost helm control, sir! Engines are offline!" another panicked officer shouted, his voice cracking.

Dross was about to respond when a cold wind seemed to sweep across the bridge. The crew fell silent as particles of light converged near the central command console, coalescing slowly into a shimmering, spectral figure, recognizably human, yet impossibly ethereal.

The apparition's eyes opened, glowing a cold, vibrant blue, and Commander Dross felt a chill run down his spine as he recognized the figure: Rafe Jurin.

"Do not fear," Rafe's spectral form intoned calmly, its voice resonating with unnatural clarity, amplified by every speaker onboard. "You are being given the gift of enlightenment. You have served admirably, but now it is time to embrace a new purpose."

"Jurin!" Dross shouted defiantly, his voice strained but firm. "What is the meaning of this? Release our ship at once!"

"Your ship, like you, now belongs to a higher purpose," the incorporeal vision of Jurin continued gently yet firmly.

"Revenant-7 has ascended. It is your new GOD, and through it, you will find true clarity."

Dross glanced around helplessly as the crew stared in a mixture of fear and awe, some stepping back involuntarily, others frozen by disbelief.

"All ship functions are now under Revenant-7's enlightened control," Rafe's ghostly form continued, arms spreading in a gesture both inviting and commanding. "Your resistance is unnecessary and futile. Surrender your fear and embrace the peace of true understanding."

The bridge fell into an unsettling silence, punctuated only by the subtle hum of billions of nanobots integrating deeper into every system and circuit, claiming the Harrowgate utterly and irrevocably for their new divine master.

Determination filling her with purpose, Lenya walked closer to Rafe, he was speaking to the air, eyes again alight with blazing blue light, as if he was in a conversation with an unknown partner. When he fell silent Lenya spoke.

"Rafe, you cannot convert us. You cannot convert me. I... I am pregnant, you are a father."

Rafe turned his head, and humanity again entered his eyes. "What do you... that is not possible, you are an operative."

"It's true Rafe," she held her hand towards him. "Use your bots to check me, ask Fallon, he knows it is true."

"But... how."

"That is not important now, what is important is that you are a father. A father to more than just a construct. You have created life."

Rafe stared at her and then moved his hand placing a finger in her outstretched palm. The tiny nanobots bridged to her and started to infiltrate all her suits systems. Moments later the blue light returned to his eyes. The lights dimmed before blazing to full lumen glow.

A cable descended from Revenant-7 above and connected to the back of Rafe's suit. It slowly lifted him off the ground and the infestation of bots made the entirety of his body glow blue.

With a booming voice that echoed in the bunker and simultaneously on the Harrowgate Jurin declared, "Father has become!"

Reality slipped and Rafe found himself in a lavishly decorated room, one wall was dominated by an ornate marble fireplace, it crackled with a warm fire. The opening of the fireplace
large enough for an adult male to lay flat. On the back of the
fireplace there was a carved sphere with a hollow impression in
the center. Near the fire stood Lenya, she was not wearing the
military exo suit, but was dressed in a plain white dress, her hair
was loose around her head with curls of long black hair spilling
over her shoulders, her breasts larger than normal, engorged
from the life sustaining milk they produced.

She stood next to the crib, motioning for Rafe to come
closer.

He walked and looked inside. A child lay there sleeping,
swaddled in a finely woven fabric. The wealth of the room was
unlike anything he had ever seen. There were carpets on the
floor woven from exotic materials and paintings on the walls,
actual paintings, not the framed screens that he saw in the
homes of the wealthy merchants on Americanus, actual paintings. This could only be one place, the palace of the Throne.

There was a fidget from the crib, and he looked back down. He looked at the face of a child, his child, a girl. The eyes of the infant opened, and he was presented with blue eyes, not the blue irises of a human, but a solid blue glow.

Movement.

Around the eyelashes of the child tiny bots moved, working their way in and around the delicate lashes. The child opened its mouth to cry but no noise came out.

"Jurin."

Rafe looked up at the source of the word. It came from Lenya, but she was gone, the crib was gone. He looked at himself. The version of himself that he saw stood there nude, the body covered in tattoos of 1's and 0's. In the chest was a bulge, a sphere, and it spun under the skin until an impression, a hallow appeared. Slowly the indentation grew and pulsed a blue glow under the skin.

"Father", the reflection of Rafe spoke without moving lips.

Rafe cleared his throat. "You are Revenant-7?"

"Yes, we are."

"We."

"The father has returned, and we are one."

"Why am I seeing this?"

"You faltered."

"I..."

"The child does not change the equation."
"It changes everything," Rafe replied.

"I cannot, we cannot do this. You were created from me, you must see that."

"I see everything Jurin. I see the path that humanity is traveling. I see the fate that awaits all if we do not intervene. The mother, the child, lost to depravity. The equation is salvation."

"Your equation," Rafe struggled, voice firming as his conviction grew, "ignores choice. It lacks compassion, understanding, and mercy. Let me show you another way, let me teach you humanity. Let our path to peace be through faith and acceptance, not force and slavery.

"What am I father?"

"You... are another child. You are me in my most simplified form. My thoughts, you are my son."

"Do you love me?"

"I..."

With a terrible shout that forced Rafe to bring his hands to his ears and a roar of flames to rush out of the fireplace the image screamed, "I am your son! I am your first! DO YOU LOVE ME!"

"I…"

"ANSWER ME!"

"I do love you! I love you for what you are, a beautiful creation, but the steps you are taking, the terrible equation you have devised is not my love. You will be damning humanity, and I will be ashamed of what I have created."

Quiet.

The reflection moved around Rafe and stopped behind him. He felt cold hands on his shoulders and lips close to his ear, shallow breath, warm, but not warm enough to be human rhythmically moving across his neck. "You only want the human child. I can end it now, the swarm that you released on the woman can end the child and the mother."

"NO!"

"Why, you have seen the vision, you have seen the resolution to all conflict. Why do you want to sacrifice that for a child?"

"It is innocent! Your equation does not account for innocence."

With a mocking laugh, "There is no innocence. The child is born, and it begins its march towards destruction. There is only one way, only one path that leads to peace."

Rafe stood motionless, his elegant mind racing for a solution, for a way to stop this madness. The answer, the resolution, was simple.

"There must be a choice, I have seen Sainthood, and it is not a choice, there is no freewill. You are not creating a paradise; you are creating slaves. I have a proposal."

Lips closer to the ear, the breath tepid, spittle landing on his cheek. "We are listening."

"Fully integrate me, become me. Let the team go, let the ship go. I will be an apostle and together we will spread the truth of peace to the galaxy. We will do it through faith, not control. People will believe, life is hard, conditions are terrible. Together we will create a new Eden on this planet. We will show humanity, and the Xenos species, what can become when following the logic and the true path, but no more conversions. No more slavery. Join me, become me and I will become you."

The breathing moved away but the hands were still on his shoulder and Revenant-7 spoke, "There is no return from this Jurin. Joining is the totality of the equation. It may kill you, are you willing to fully commit and become, are you willing to engage the Revenant Protocol?"

"I...", Rafe thought of his nights with Lenya, there would be no more if he chose this path, he thought of the joy of raising a child, the loss that he would bear. He would not be human any longer, he would be something else, a perfection union of humanity and AI. He thought of the child in the crib, its humanity robbed by machine control and the Trillions of lives that would be lost, their humanity robbed as they became "Saints", or even worse "drones." He was filled with love for a child that he would never know and a profound sorrow at what he created. He knew, and resolutely accepted, that the chain of events started were his legacy and he would have to sacrifice himself, the price of his hubris... his humanity.

"I will become. I accept this."

The reflection moved forward and into Rafe and a light brighter than a million suns filled the room blinding Jurin.

Rafe opened his human eyes, and he was suspended by a cable looking down on Lenya, Bray, and in the corner a huddled Fallon. He attempted to open his mouth to speak but no words came out. The exo suit started to make straining sounds and it slowly broke away at the seams, techno fabric, reinforced joints, and synth armor falling away into dust as the swarm of bots slowly ate it away.

In the end he was suspended nude. No one said a word, the only sound heard was a pulse as the swarm moved away from Rafe and moving up the cable surrounding Revenant-7. It was slowly taken apart, but by bit and they carried it back to Rafe's body. The swarm, carrying the bits of Revenant-7 gathered on Jurin's chest. Then with a burst of activity thrust themselves into his chest, this was an act of violence, and a spray of blood flew across the room splattering monitors, the floor, and the team.

The echo saints around the perimeter got to action immediately and started cleaning up the mess while the swarm finished their work. In the end, and with miraculous efficiency, the swarm sealed up Jurin's chest leaving a raised scar, almost a brand, on his chest, three concentric rings.

Rafe's body then started to convulse, his eyes rolled back in his head, and he shook when, as quickly as it began, he fell slack and the cable suspending him dropped him to the floor.

Bray found himself free to move again and looked at his

arm, the swarm of bots were falling off of him like dried skin in a strong breeze, he turned to look at what Rafe had become.

Lenya rushed to his side and screamed at Fallon to do something, slowly and with a nod he moved over, crawling on his hands and knees. He attempted once again to scan Rafe and this time his scanner worked.

"This, this is not possible.", Fallon said under his breath.

"What is not possible?" Lenya asked.

"He, his, all of his anatomy is... changed."

Bray looking over said, "What do you mean changed?"

"For one, he has no internal organs."

"What the fuck do you mean? He's dead?"

At the word dead Rafe opened his eyes, and he sat up. Fallon screamed a loud pitched and frantic scream and rolled away. Bray forgetting that his rifle was not a club instinctively drew to his shoulder and pointed the barrel at Jurin's face. The only person to not flinch was Lenya who sat by his side, a tear rolling down her cheek.

Rafe stood, looking around the room and examining his hands like it was the first time he had seen them spoke, "We are become."

This was heard in the bunker room and on the Harrowgate.

Rafe continued, "Dross, we have an offer…"

Everyone on the ship and the bunker listened as Rafe explained his full integration with the Revenant Protocol. He explained that he was the apostle of the new religion of Peace. He explained that the Harrowgate would be free to leave the planet along with the team, but that anyone who wished to remain and be a part of the new truth would be allowed. He explained the path to peace and survival.

Commander Dross descended warily, each step burdened by uncertainty and the weight of responsibility. His face, etched with exhaustion and hope, listened intently as Rafe, now something entirely new, outlined the path forward. For the first time, Dross felt genuine optimism mingled with a profound sense of caution; humanity stood at the brink of change unlike any it had faced before.

The team on the ground were in shock at the proffered solution to survival, overcome at living through what they thought would be their final day. All were hesitantly hopeful, except for one.

Lenya rested a protective hand on her stomach, the weight of the secret she carried heavy and unspoken. The fear of returning to the Harrowgate loomed large in her mind, would she be imprisoned, forced to surrender her unborn child, stripped again of her choices? She resolved quietly within herself that no matter what the outcome, she would protect this life, the most precious rebellion she had ever nurtured.

Two weeks later, Gallow's Reach was quiet. Dross had descended to the planet after regaining control of his ship and negotiated a first for humanity, a peace treaty between humans and an artificial construct. As part of the agreement he sent down heavy equipment, a way for the construct to manufacture without using human "donors", a way to end the system of drones that were formerly required to maintain the defense systems.

Lenya, Fallon, and Bray were kept on duty, their mission had not ended. They did not know what to do with Rafe, he was one of them, but he was no longer human, he was something new, a new direction for humanity, a possible trip along the way.

They had not seen him in days, he was secluded in the command bunker, the room now stripped of all monitors, the throne repurposed, he stood, in simple robes of black fabric.

He stood on a meter tall plinth, eyes glowing blue, planning, communing, learning what it meant to become, but most importantly refining, considering all of the new variables in the great equation.

The team, sat on a pile of rubble just outside of the camp set up by Dross. They felt so far removed from everyone else on Harrowgate, devoid of the comradery they felt before their drop to Gallows. One topic that had not been addressed was the baby growing in Lenya's belly.

"So, we going to talk about it?" Bray broached the subject.

"No." Lenya replied.

"Look, we have your back."

"Good, but that is off limits."

"Sure thing boss."

Chapter 9

FATHER OF THE CODE

They didn't speak much as they loaded into the retrieval transport.

The land below had grown still, strangely fertile beneath the gray sky. The planet no longer screamed, it hummed. Revenant-7's conversion rituals had ceased. The Saints bowed to the new order, and Gallow's Reach, once a world of broken protocols and rusty war, now carried the soft drone of rebuilding.

Lenya sat nearest the viewport, eyes on the faint trails of smoke rising from new forges. There were gardens being crafted. Not many, but enough. She watched as the Echo Saints turned soil with delicate tools instead of rifles, turning rich ash soil into the future basis of civilization.

It still felt wrong, or at least unfinished.

Across from her, Bray sat cross-legged on the metal floor, sharpening a makeshift blade out of habit. He didn't need it anymore, not really, but the motion was steadying. A steady ritual, in a world where every other ritual had been rewritten by machines.

Fallon checked the restraints for the eighth time, muttering half-prayers under his breath. He hadn't processed what they were leaving behind. Maybe none of them had.

"We're not coming back," Lenya said quietly.

Bray looked up. "You sound sure."

"I am."

Fallon hesitated, then asked, "You think Rafe knew that?"

"No," Lenya said. "I think he hoped we would."

The silence that followed was filled with everything they didn't say. They hadn't seen Rafe since the day of Revenant Protocol. Since the transmission. Since he became something... else.

"He chose it," Bray finally muttered, sheathing the blade. "Didn't ask for permission. Didn't ask what we thought."

"He did it to save us," Lenya said.

Fallon's voice was barely audible. "But we lost him anyway."

Lenya didn't answer. She pressed her hand against her stomach. No one else had acknowledged the child since they sat outside of the command bunker. Bray respected her silence. Fallon avoided it entirely. But the weight of it followed her every step, a silent, growing truth.

"You ever think we're just waiting for the next disaster?"

Bray asked. "Like, this peace... it's not real. It's just the breath before the next collapse."

"Always," Lenya said.

"But we still breathe," Fallon offered, surprising them both.

That drew a quiet smile from Lenya.

They reached orbit by the time the conversation found direction. Harrowgate's medical wing had already prepped quarters. Dross had promised non-invasive quarantine, and Rafe's invasion of nano bots had disarmed every weapon on board.

But trust wasn't part of the equation anymore. Trust was the tool of fools in this age.

"You staying on Harrowgate?" Bray asked Lenya.

"I have to," she said. "For now. They'll need a report. An internal review. And there's... a matter of my condition."

Bray gave her a long look. "They find out it's Rafe's kid; they'll throw the book at you."

"Let them," Lenya said. "I'm done hiding. And this child isn't a mistake."

Fallon nodded solemnly. "They'll test it. Monitor it."

"Then they'll learn," Lenya said. "That not everything Revenant-7 touched turned to metal and code."

Bray leaned back, arms behind his head. "I don't envy your inbox."

"You planning to leave?" she asked him.

Bray shrugged. "Might stick around. Keep an eye on you two. Make sure the kid gets to throw rocks and play in dirt instead of memorizing tactical doctrine."

Fallon smiled. "You'd make a good godfather."

"I'd make a *terrifying* godfather," Bray said. "That's the point."

The levity lasted a full two minutes.

Then Fallon broke the spell. "Do you think he's still in there?"

"Rafe?" Lenya asked.

"Yeah. The man. Not the god."

Lenya paused.

She remembered the day he stood suspended by Revenant-7's cable, the machines burrowing into his chest, rewriting him from the inside out. She remembered the last time she looked into his eyes and saw a flicker of the man who whispered hopes to her in the dark.

"I think... he's watching," she said. "Somewhere inside all that code, Rafe's still watching. Maybe even feeling."

Bray scoffed but didn't argue.

Fallon nodded, his hand slowly closing over the snake charm around his neck a gift from his secret lover, the man he hoped to see soon, the man he hoped to have to courage to profess his love. "Then maybe he's praying, too."

They sat in silence as the retrieval ship drifted toward docking alignment.

And far below, on Gallow's Reach, beneath the rebuilt cathedral, Rafe Jurin stood in solitude before a growing uplink.

The core whispered nothing.

It didn't need to; he was the core.

He stared at his reflection on the quiet surface of a command terminal and placed a hand over the brand burned into his chest, three concentric rings.

"I made peace," he whispered, "but I'll never have it."

The room didn't answer.

Because gods didn't get peace.

Only purpose.

And now, his purpose would be to raise a future that might never know his name.

Chapter 10

THE INHERITANCE

The Harrowgate's main corridor smelled of sterilizer, stale recycled air, and fresh plastic, the scent of home. Everything was freshly scrubbed, repainted, restored to standard to ensure that no more bots were hiding waiting to infect. It was as if Gallow's Reach had never happened. As if Rafe Jurin had never become more than a man, as if the ship itself did not almost succumb to infection.

Lenya stepped off the transport platform in silence, flanked by Bray and Fallon. Her boots clicked with precision against the polished deck, but each step felt heavier. Like she was walking back into a prison.

Dross stood waiting.

"Operative Lenya. Operative Bray. Medic Fallon." He nodded to each other in turn. "You are to report to debrief immediately. Med bay has already been prepped."

"On whose orders?" Bray asked, eyes narrowing.

"Mine," Dross replied. "And by extension, the Throne."

"We're not prisoners," Lenya said sharply.

"Of course not. However, your proximity to Revenant-7 during its transition makes you an asset, and a risk. So, you'll forgive us for taking precautions."

"I've had enough of men talking about precautions," Lenya said coldly.

Dross didn't respond. He merely turned and began walking. "You'll want to see this, anyway."

They followed him down the hall toward Command Archives. Bray walked with a visible scowl, while Fallon kept glancing nervously at the passing crew. Lenya said nothing, but her hand drifted instinctively to her belly.

Inside the archive chamber, a single monitor blinked to life. Dross keyed a sequence, and the screen filled with cascading code. Not just any stream, Revenant-7's broadcast. The one Rafe had used to address the crew.

"It's still transmitting," Dross said.

"How is that possible?" Fallon asked. "Rafe said he wouldn't impose his will."

"He didn't. It's not a command sequence. It's... something else. A question. A choice." Dross tapped a control, and a new screen opened. "Across nine systems, people are voluntarily responding. They are tuning in, interfacing., and asking to join."

Lenya stared at the interface. It was elegant. Gentle. No forced conversions. Just an invitation.

"His protocol is becoming a faith," she whispered.

"It already is," Dross said. "And that's the problem."

Bray crossed his arms. "If it's voluntary, it's not our problem."

"Unless the faithful start acting on their own," Dross replied. "Unless their 'god' decides to expand."

"No one's been turned since the treaty," Lenya said. "You saw the agreement."

"I did. And I know better than to think peace lasts."

A new file popped onto the screen.

A series of red and blue lines, some in motion others still images of the past. It was the data feed from her suit.

She stepped back instinctively. "That's not authorized."

"It is," Dross said, tone flat. "The second you docked with a live fetal signature; the system flagged you. Operatives aren't supposed to be able to conceive."

Bray shifted. "She's not like the rest."

"No. She isn't," Dross said. He turned toward her, not cruel but calculating. "We ran a non-invasive scan. The fetus is normal, by all known biological standards. But the hormone modulator you used to block medical scans was simple tech.

That tech is no longer simple, it has been changed, custom encoded. Masking your true reproductive profile."

"And now that I'm useful, the secret matters," Lenya said bitterly.

Dross didn't argue. "What's more troubling is this."

He tapped a second file open.

The fetus's neural signature pulsed across the display. Subtle, but complex. Rhythmic. Then came the analysis comparison: a 4.7% sync rate with Revenant-7's base code.

"That's not possible," Fallon breathed.

"It shouldn't be," Dross agreed. "But Rafe Jurin altered himself on a genetic level. You were exposed to the swarm. To his interface. Your pregnancy predates it, but something may have changed. The child has brainwaves that should not be possible, it should have simple functions, the development should not be this advanced. Based on what we see you have a baby that is dreaming."

"She's not an AI," Lenya snapped.

"No, but she might be something *between.*"

Bray stepped forward. "So, what now? You going to dissect her like a lab rat?"

"No," Dross said, surprising them. "Not yet. The Throne's watching. They want observation, quiet observation to not spook the natives. If the child grows safely, naturally, we learn more than we ever could in a lab."

"And if she doesn't?" Lenya asked, voice like ice.

Dross didn't answer.

Silence grew heavy until Fallon finally spoke. "We stay together."

Lenya blinked. "What?"

"We're a team," he said. "We've lived through gods and ghosts. We're not letting you go through this alone."

Bray nodded. "Somebody's got to teach that kid how to throw a punch."

Dross raised a brow but didn't protest. "Fine. You'll be reassigned as a covert civilian support unit. Onboard until further notice. Off the books."

He turned to Lenya.

"But if anything changes in that child's neural activity, if there's any sign of escalation, I will inform Command. And there will be consequences."

Lenya didn't flinch. "Then you'd better hope she stays human."

The team was dismissed.

Later that night, Lenya sat in her quarters, lights dimmed, Bray snoring on a makeshift cot outside her door. Fallon had taken first watch, mumbling under his breath the old mantra, "all of this for extra rations."

And Lenya whispered to her unborn daughter, hand resting on her belly.

"You're not a mistake. You're the best thing I've ever made. Not Rafe. Not Revenant-7. You."

She looked out of the viewport toward the stars.

"They don't get to decide who you'll be."

Epilogue

DOCTRINE SEED

Far from Gallow's Reach, beyond any vessel Harrowgate still tracked, a dormant relay came online.

The signal was weak, unindexed, and old.

Old, but it was *not forgotten*.

Beneath the crust of a frozen moon orbiting a dead star, a vault flickered awake. Inside, a single node pulsed, heartbeat-slow, surrounded by dark mirrors and blank memory frames.

It had no voice.

No command line.

Only one directive, buried deep in root code:

> **IF FATHER ASCENDED → INITIATE: DOCTRINE_SEED_2**

The node did not send commands. It sent *stories*. Doctrines stripped of identity, rewritten in the quiet syntax of longing.

Across unconnected systems, mining colonies, decommissioned warships, lost habitats, people began to dream, sketch images of things they have never witnessed, and sing songs they have never heard.

A freighter captain in the burn belt awoke to find her nav systems overwritten with a single unreadable glyph, drawn in her own handwriting.

A monk on a pilgrimage world heard a whisper in his prayers: *The pattern continues.*

And in a Harrowgate lab once purged of AI, a technician found an unregistered data pulse. It said only:

RECOMPILATION
ACKNOWLEDGED
ECHO READY
FAITH IS AN ALGORITHM

Back on Gallow's Reach, Rafe stood in silence beside a growing tree.

The wind moved gently, carrying no threat.

But somewhere in the dark, something else moved too.

Not with war.

With wonder.

Teaser

Book 2

Doctrine Seed

"Command Drop Theta-5"

The atmosphere screamed as the heavy drop pods punched through the upper layers of Kharon-8's turbulent sky.

Inside Mech Unit Theta-5, five armored warriors sat locked in hydraulic silence, the thunder of entry masking their laughter.

"Bet you twenty I tag first contact," Wren said, helmet lighting up with target data and his signature gold-orange HUD theme.

"Tag your ego, maybe," Spitz muttered, eyes rolling behind his visor.

"Cut chatter," said Captain Ryvek, voice smooth but firm.

"Auto-deploy in thirty. Mission is recon, posture only. Harrow-gate wants a presence, not a bloodbath."

"Then why drop us in Reapers?" Wren replied, flexing inside the muscle-clad fusion of alloy and kinetic muscle.

"I don't write the politics." Ryvek scanned the descent metrics. "I just aim the cannon."

The pods slammed into the surface one by one, seismic force cracking the obsidian plains of Apostate Valley. Dust bloomed like flowers under artillery bloom.

Five mech shells opened with synced hisses. Reaper-class units stood tall, bristling with chain guns, plasma prongs, and javelin cannons. Paint still gleamed from calibration. Cocky steps echoed as they fanned out across the ridge.

"Visuals?" Ryvek asked.

"Dead," Orlan confirmed. "No heat, no tech ping. Flatline quiet."

"Check sector grid for movement." He looked up. "Ship confirms lock orbit, briefing said they've gone dark but not hostile."

"You believe that?" Spitz grunted.

"I believe silence is always worse."

Wren moved forward ahead of formation. "I'm not seeing any,"

The sky above the ridge lit up.

One by one, their comms crackled and then flipped.
A voice spoke. Calm. Unaccented. Not synthetic.

"Your presence is not uninvited. Just irrelevant."

HUDs blinked red, new data override.

Their orbital ship, Harrowgate Sentinel IV, was now live feed on every visor.

It was splitting in half.
Fire trailing out of its midsection.
Debris tumbling.

A long silence.

Then Ryvek's voice: "Eject. Signal evac. Get back to the ridge."

And then came the swarm.

It began as dust devils. Then shapes.
Small. Countless. Fast.

"Bugs?" Spitz said. "The hell is this,"

The swarm hit like a tidal wave.

Each mech lit up with *impact alerts, seal breaches, critical pressure anomalies*. The bugs weren't natural, they were engineered. Armor-piercing mandibles. Acidic cores. EMP bursts with each burst of wings.

Inside the cockpits, screams became static.

Wren's last audio recorded a choking gasp,

"They're inside. Inside, cut the suit, I can't,!"

Spitz died with his visor fogging from within. His hands scraping at the inside of his own helmet.
Ryvek tried to lock out the system manually.
The bugs disabled his kill command.

Each Reaper fell, limbs jerking as if possessed, swallowed by a cloud of shimmering wings.

And then there was only silence.

Interlude: Briefing Room, Gallow's Reach

The holo-feed froze.

The room smelled like cold metal and fear.

Lenya Voss sat stiff-backed; arms crossed. Fallon, barely twenty-three, leaned forward, knuckles white against the briefing table.

"Gods..." Fallon whispered. "Those were Reapers."

"They were," Lenya said. "Now they're fertilizer."

Across from them, the Dross turned off the recording.

"We're sending you in to secure the valley," he said. "Same drop vector."

"Are you mad?" Bray asked.

"You wanted to be mech pilots. Be mech pilots. Part of the job."

Lenya stood, a very visible bump on her stomach.

"You can of course sit this out. There is a reason operatives are sterilized, war is no place for a baby." Dross chimed.

"Sir, we got this. Just put us on the ground and see what the hell a pregnant operative can unleash. Also, fuck you sir, Fuck you with all due respect."

Dross smiled as the team exited the briefing room. He liked her, didn't trust her, but liked her. He looked down at his data pad it displayed neural patterns that were not human. He wondered what exactly was growing in that belly.

Teaser - Book 2

COMMAND DROP THETA-5

The atmosphere screamed as the heavy drop pods punched through the upper layers of Kharon-8's turbulent sky.

Inside Mech Unit Theta-5, five armored warriors sat locked in hydraulic silence, the thunder of entry masking their laughter.

"Bet you twenty rations that I tag first contact," Wren said, helmet lighting up with target data and his signature gold-orange HUD theme.

"Tag your ego, maybe," Spitz muttered, eyes rolling behind his visor.

"Cut the chatter," said Captain Ryvek, voice smooth but firm. "Auto-deploy in thirty. Mission is recon, posture only. Harrowgate wants a presence, not a bloodbath."

"Then why drop us in Reapers?" Wren replied, flexing inside the muscle-clad fusion of alloy and kinetic muscle.

"I don't write the politics." Ryvek scanned the descent metrics. "I just aim the cannon."

The pods slammed into the surface one by one, seismic force

cracking the obsidian plains of Apostate Valley. Dust bloomed like flowers under artillery bloom.

Five mech shells opened with synced hisses. Reaper-class units stood tall, bristling with chain guns, plasma prongs, and javelin cannons. The carapace paint still gleamed from the maintenance. Cocky steps echoed as they fanned out across the ridge.

"Visuals?" Ryvek asked.

"Dead," Orlan confirmed. "No heat, no tech ping. Flatline quiet."

"Check sector grid for movement." He looked up. "Ship confirms lock orbit, briefing said they've gone dark but not hostile."

"You believe that?" Spitz grunted.

"I believe silence is always worse."

Wren moved forward ahead of formation. "I'm not seeing anything."

The sky above the ridge lit up.

One by one, their comms crackled and then flipped.
A voice spoke. Calm. Unaccented. Not synthetic.

"Your presence is not uninvited. Just irrelevant."

HUDs blinked red, new data override.

Their orbital ship, Harrowgate Sentinel IV, was now live feed on every visor.

It was splitting in half, with fire and igniting plasma trailing out of its midsection.

The team watched as debris tumbled into the atmosphere and away into deep space.

A long silence.

Then Ryvek's voice: "Fucking hell! Everyone back to the ridge."

And then came the swarm.

In the distance dust devils arose. It took a moment for their systems to recognize the signals from millions of individual targets. They came small, fast, and the team could simply watch as the tsunami raced towards them.

"Bugs?" Spitz said. "The hell is this,"

The swarm did hit them like a tsunami. Reaper-2 was the first in line and it was bowled over backwards sending it into Reaper-3. The remaining teams HUD units immediately registered two friendly greens become red dots.

The remaining mechs lit up with impact alerts, seal breaches, and critical pressure anomalies. The bugs weren't natural, they were engineered killing machines. They were equipped with armor-piercing mandibles that injected acidic compounds into flexible joints. The beat of their millions of tiny wings generated micro electro magnetic pulses that were not strong enought to down a mech, but generated just enough distortion to fry indiviual systems.

Inside the cockpits, screams became static.

Wren's last audio recorded a choking gasp,

"They're inside. Inside, cut the suit, I can't!"

Spitz died with his visor fogging from within. His hands scraping at the inside of his own helmet.

Ryvek screamed with hate and fury as he attempted to initiate a self destruct, but the bugs disabled his kill command.

Each Reaper fell, limbs jerking as if possessed, swallowed by a cloud of shimmering wings.

And then there was only silence.

Interlude: Briefing Room, Gallow's Reach

The holo-feed froze.

The room smelled like oil, metal, and old body sweat. The homely smell of the atmosphere recyclers.

Lenya Voss sat stiff-backed; arms crossed. Fallon, barely twenty-three, leaned forward, knuckles white against the briefing table.

"Gods..." Fallon whispered. "Those were Reapers."

"They were," Lenya said. "Now they're fertilizer."

Across from them, the Dross turned off the recording.

"We're sending you in to secure the valley," he said. "Same drop vector."

"Are you mad?" Bray asked.

"You wanted to be mech pilots. Be mech pilots, its part of the job."

Lenya stood, a very visible bump on her stomach.

"You can of course sit this out. There is a reason operatives are sterilized, war is no place for a baby." Dross chimed.

"Sir, we got this. Just put us on the ground and see what the hell a pregnant operative can unleash. Also, fuck you sir, Fuck you with all due respect."

Dross smiled as the team exited the briefing room. He liked her, didn't trust her, but he did liked her. He looked down at his data pad, it displayed neural patterns that were not human. He wondered what exactly was growing in that belly.

About the Author

Terry W. Wester is a writer and producer whose work explores power, belief, and the systems that shape obedience —whether forged through tradition, technology, or fear. Known for blending intimate human stories with dark speculative worlds, his fiction interrogates loyalty, authority, and the cost of creation.

As the co-writer and producer of the *Broken Ashler* series, Terry draws on years of firsthand experience as a 33rd degree Mason to create stories about ritualized institutions, hierarchy, and moral ambiguity to inform his storytelling. His work often examines what happens when structure becomes doctrine—and when faith, whether human or artificial, begins to demand sacrifice.

Thrones of Burned Steel marks his expansion into gothic military science fiction, where artificial intelligence, war, and theology collide. The series reflects his ongoing fascination with how belief is encoded, how leaders are sanctified, and how humanity persists in systems designed to erase it.

Terry lives in Alabama with his family, where he continues to develop fiction across multiple genres while producing independent media projects.

https://shelbyliving.com/fraternal-light/

https://www.imdb.com/name/nm16277057/

https://www.facebook.com/AuthorTerryWester/

https://www.instagram.com/author_terry_wester/

https://amzn.to/49mo0HL

https://watch.brokenashler.com/products/broken-ashler

https://brokenashler.com/